Rejected

Nina Clust

Contents

1.The Rejection

Hey lovelies

Welcome to the first chap.

You're a beautiful person if you're reading this.___________________
____Alyssa's POV

It's so soft.

So comfy I thought as I stretched on the comfy bed.

But my bed wasn't this comfy. I thought and immediately sat up.

Damn

I thought as I looked around the large dark painted room.

This wasn't my room.

I looked beside me and slightly jumped as I saw who it was sleeping peacefully beside me. I placed a palm over my mouth as I tried to muffle my scream.

I couldn't believe I was here right now.

What the heck happened last night?

Then little by little, the memories came flooding in.

There was a party here at the pack house last night. The Alpha was Celebrating his eighteenth birthday. I was serving the drinks and I accidentally bumped into him.

He looked at me wide eyes and called me his 'mate'.

He was intoxicated I knew it but yet I let lust and greed take over me and I went into this room with him and let him have his way with me....

Oh no. What have I done?

Wait, why am I being scared about this? He is my mate. Isn't it normal for this to happen.

The internal battle with myself was cut short when Axel stretched beside me and rubbed his eyes while sitting up.

"Ugh, I have a bad headache." He said holding his head. He still didn't know I was sitting there beside him.

While he kept groaning, I took my time to admire his god like body. How could a man be so handsome?

From him silk blonde hair to his dark grey orbs. His well structured face and pointed nose, everything about him screamed perfection.

I was yet again cut from my train of thoughts when he suddenly snapped his head towards me.

"Alyssa? What the fuck are you doing in my bed and my room?!" He said, giving me a once over.

I immediately felt conscious and pulled the covers closer to my bare chest.

"I asked you a damned question!" He yelled again rising up to his feet. I shrieked at the tone of his voice and looked down at the bed.

"N... nothing. You...you brought me here." I stuttered timidly.

"And why would I do that?!" He barked yet again. Did he really not remember anything from last night?

I looked up to meet his scrutinizing gaze and shivered.

"Be... because I'm your mate." I squeaked but being the Alpha wolf he was, he definitely heard me.

He seemed to be hit by realization as he went silent for a while and then scrunched his eyebrows in confusion.

"This can't be." He said.

"The goddess must have made some kind of mistake in our pairing. You can't possibly be my mate." He bit out and I felt my chest tighten.

My mate didn't want me.

All my dreams and hopes of meeting the one that'll love me for infinity gone down the drain just like that.

"I'm going to reject you." He blurted.

"You're no better than the useless omegas out there." He continued and I tugged at my chest.

"I Axel Jameson Braun reject you Alyssa Megara Brown as my mate and Luna of this pack." He said and walked out.

I felt my entire world crumbling right there and then. I couldn't bear the pain anymore and I burst into fit of tears.

How could my mate reject me?

I understand that I'm a weakling no one in the pack associates with but I was still his mate. How could he do that?

My mind flooded with the memories of the past.

When I first lost my mother at the wolf clash ten years back when she was trying to save me to when my father died three years ago trying to save me from a fire.

I was the cause of my parents death. The reason why everyone hated me.

I was the Beta's daughter but now I was just the girl who helped around in the pack house.

Even the Alpha loathed me. I was the cause of his Beta's death after all. His son who just happened to be my mate also hated the mere sight of me.

We used to be very close friends but after what happened, he just distanced himself from me. Everyone did.

More tears flowed down my cheeks as I thought about my miserable life.

The only one I had was no one.

I was all alone in this cruel world. What was the point of living anyway.

I've only held on for the past three years because of my mate and my wolf who was yet to come.

But now my mate rejected me and if I eventually get my wolf in seven months time, she'll do just the same after all we didn't have a mate.

The mere thought of that digged daggers into my heart and made me cry more.

Who did I have I have in this world then?

I carefully climbed out of the bed and picked up my clothes which were all over the floor.

I winced at the pain I was feeling and more tears went down my eyes as memories of last night flooded my brain.

He looked at me so lovingly for the first time in three years. But all that was gone by the crack of dawn.

I put on the last of my clothing and sneaked out of the room silently praying to the moon goddess that no one should see me walking out of Axel's room.

I successfully reached my room and locked the door behind me before landing on my small bed.

I looked at the wall beside me, filled with photos of my parents.

My mom's pretty smile as my dad looked at her so affectionately.

Was I never going to have that too?

I sighed as I sat up on the bed.

I don't think I should be here anymore.

I had no purpose and no one here in this pack. My mate already rejected me. It would be for the best if I left.

Everyone would like that too.....

>>>>>>>>>>>>

2.Goodbye

POV

When I woke up and saw Alyssa beside me, all I felt was fury.

Why was she in my bed half naked? What did we do last night?

Though I had an idea, I didn't want to admit it and that's why I yelled at her.

I could see she was scared by my tone but I didn't fucking care.

Then she said I brought her there and that she was my mate.

I couldn't believe my ears. Alyssa was my mate?

Mason my wolf I just got yesterday felt happy about that fact but I wasn't.

He whimpered and queried me when I rejected our mate but I didn't pay attention to him.

If only he had been with me three years ago to watch the life leave the eyes of the one man I admired even more than my own father all because of his bratty daughter.

That day when Beta Wilson died in the fire trying to rescue Alyssa who started the fire in the first place.

Whenever I remember that event, I feel nothing but anger and hatred towards Alyssa.

True we were childhood friends and grew up together and there was even a point in my life when I fell in love with her but those feelings died the day I watch her father die.

Her father was my hero. A man I so much looked up to.

Back to the present. I rejected Alyssa down flat and I could see the hurt in her eyes. I felt a tug in my heart but I ignored it and walked out of the room before I'd change my mind.

No doubt a small part of me still loved Alyssa but the grieve of her father's death was still there and it overshadowed that little love I had left for her.

I went to the kitchen for breakfast and saw Mom and Clara the pack house's cook there.

"Good morning Son." Mom greeted me smiling. She was munching on nachos while Clara was cooking.

"Morning Mom." I said as I placed a kiss on her forehead and sat beside her.

"Good morning Alpha." Clara said and brought a plate of omelettes before me.

I nodded and her and Mom turned to me.

"How does it feel to be eighteen? I'm so excited for you son. After your graduation next month, you'll finally take over the Alpha position from your father." She said grinning from ear to ear.

"Of course Mom. I'm also excited about that." I said and put a piece of omelette in my mouth.

Just then Bianca my younger sister stepped in with her white puppy in her arms.

"Hello family. Morning Clara." She beamed and I rolled my eyes. Mom smiled at her and Clara greeted back.

"Come join us for breakfast dear. Don't let Sara into the kitchen. I always tell you." Mom said referring to Bianca's puppy who was now on the floor, licking it's fur.

"She's just too sweet. I need to carry her around." Bianca claimed as she sat beside me.

"Morning brother." She said, smiling weirdly at me.

"What?". I snapped and she groaned.

"Always so uptight." She murmured as Clara placed a plate of omelettes before her.

"Later we're all going shopping for your brother's forthcoming Alpha ceremony. Alyssa would be coming as well cos we'll need many hands. Speaking of Alyssa, where is she cos I haven't seen her all morning." Mom said speaking to no one in particular.

I tensed at the mention of Alyssa.

I haven't told anyone yet about her being my mate.

Alyssa's POV

I had managed to pack a few of my things including my parents' pictures into a duffel bag as I didn't own any luggages and even if I did, I wouldn't want to draw attention to myself.

I took a final look around the room I grew up in. Once upon a time, this room was filled with all the happiness in the world but right now it was just dull.

I sighed as I hoisted the duffel bag up my shoulders and walked out of the room.

I went out through the front door as I knew everyone would be in the kitchen.

I immediately hid behind a wall on seeing Alpha Benjamin, soon to be Beta Austin and soon to be gamma Jason walking in from the front door.

They seemed to be in a deep conversation about something but I was too tensed about them seeing me to listen to whatever they were talking about.

Suddenly Alpha Benjamin stopped walking and the other two did the same.

"What is it Alpha?" Austin asked.

"I smell someone around here. Whoever it is is hiding in a corner." Alpha Benjamin said and my heart raced.

I shut my eyes tight and held my breath, praying to the moon goddess for him not to notice me as I was right behind them.

If they should turn, they'll be looking straight at me.

"Haha. I'm sure there's no one here Alpha. It's just your subconscious." Jason said and Alpha Benjamin nodded thoughtfully before proceeding up the stairs.

I sighed in relief as they left.

That was a close call

I thought as I pushed myself away from the wall. Clutching to my bag tightly, I walked out the front door and looked back at the place I've grown to call my home.

But I had to remind myself that this wasn't a home. It was a place that left me with so many sad memories.

Although I had a lot of sweet memories as well. Memories of my parents that I'll forever hold on to.

I disappeared into the thick forest and ran and ran.

Good by blue Moon pack

>>>>>>>>>>>>

Hey lovelies.

I hope your day is going great?

Pls vote and comment.

Peace

3.Rogue

You're a beautiful person if you're reading this.________________
____Alyssa's POV

My feet were hurting from the blisters that were now all over it.

I've been running for hours, I know I was already miles away from Blue moon pack but I didn't want to take any chances.

They were probably looking for me now. I wondered if anyone actually cared that I was gone anyway. They were probably happy I left after all they never wanted me to start with.

I was now standing by a small river. I had no idea where I was. I could be in another pack for all I knew and that would be a dangerous game because I could get killed right away for being a rogue.

Rogue

How did my life turn out this way? A seventeen year old girl who was once a Beta's daughter was now a rogue.

I sat by the river bank and raised my knees, leaning onto them as I watched the still waters.

I didn't know for how long I sat there just watching the river.

I was starting to get really hungry and tired. I've been running for hours without a break or even a drop of water.

It would have been easier and less lonelier if only I'd gotten my wolf already. But now I wasn't even sure if I wanted that anymore.

I immediately sat straight as I heard footsteps coming from the thick forest behind me.

I didn't have a high sense of smell or hearing like most werewolves do because I hadn't yet gotten my wolf.

I stood up and looked around but saw no one. Maybe it was just my paranoia. I thought and turned back to the river.

I should probably get going.

As I picked up my bag ready to leave, I heard voices behind me.

I wasn't here alone

As I made to run sideways, I heard a loud voice.

"Freeze or you'll regret the consequences." The male voice boomed and I stopped right on my tracks, probably looking like a deer caught in the head lights right now.

I turned around to look at the intruders. My mouth fell open as they approached me.

They were three in number and all looked devilishly handsome.

The oldest had sleek black hair and brown eyes. The other one was blonde with blue eyes and the last one had brown hair and brown eyes.

They all looked equally handsome but I couldn't help but compare them to my mate. He was definitely a million times more handsome than this trio.

Gosh am I stupid? How can I be thinking of these men that way? They were probably gonna kill me for trespassing.

"I know we're breathtaking, flower. But eyes are up here." The blonde one said smugly and I immediately snapped out of my thoughts, embarrassed.

"What's a young rogue like yourself doing in our packlands?" The first one with black hair asked.

He was also the one who stopped me from running earlier.

"I.. I-"

"Don't worry. You'll explain yourself to the Alpha. Let's go." He cut me off abruptly and grabbed my wrist harshly.

My bag fell at the impact and the blonde picked it up.

I was scared out of my mind right now.

Two things could happen.

Either they send me back home if they found out I was a runaway or I get killed.

I definitely wasn't hoping for the latter but the former wasn't as appealing either.

I just hoped their Alpha would be kind enough to let me go. I'll just go find some human city to settle in. That'd be better.

I was snapped out of my thoughts by the man dragging me. He was strong as hell and my wrist already hurt badly. No doubt it'll leave a bruise.

We eventually got to the pack house and I had to say it was marvellous.

I didn't know the name of this pack but from the look of it, it was a really peaceful pack.

I hoped the Alpha would be as peaceful as the pack.

They led me into a room and I could see a man standing front of the floor to ceiling glass window.

He was backing us so I couldn't see his face.

"Alpha. We caught a rogue." The brown haired guy spoke for the first time since I met him.

The one manhandling me finally let go of me and I rubbed at the now reddened spot around my frail wrist.

This will leave a bruise on my smooth porcelain skin.

"Leave." The Alpha said loudly making me snap my eyes to him.

The three men left, closing the door behind them.

Now it was just me and the Alpha in the room.

He finally turned to me and looked at me for sometime.

The Alpha was just as handsome as every other guy I had seen in this pack. Was it some kind of trait?

He had midnight black hair and brown eyes. Those eyes held so many emotions I couldn't tell. He was really young probably around 18 or 19.

I was feeling uncomfortable by his persistent gaze on me. We have just been like that for what felt like hours.

Suddenly he smiled making me scrunch my face in confusion.

He was a weird one.

"Sit." He said as he went to sit on his desk.

I raised an eyebrow at him but did as I was told anyway.

"I'm Alpha Miles. What's your name?" He said and I hesitated before answering.

"A.. Alyssa." I muttered.

"Beautiful." Came his reply. "What are you doing in my pack?" He asked.

"I.. I'm really sorry. I didn't know I was in a pack. I...I was just passing through. Please if you let me leave, I'll just go and cause no trouble." I ranted and he just looked at me calmly.

"You ran away from your pack." He deadpanned and my eyes widened. How did he know?

"What...but how did you-"

"It's quite obvious actually." He said and looked down at my duffel bag that the blonde had apparently left carelessly by the door.

"And you're looking all weak and tired. Plus I can't smell a wolf on you which means you're below eighteen. There's no way a wolf less young girl would trespass with the intentions of causing havoc." He said and I was amazed by his smartness.

"Oh." I said.

"So let's make a deal." He said smiling sweetly. He was the complete opposite of Axel. He was more open, observant and friendlier.

"What deal?"

"I'll accept you into my pack and keep you safe from whatever it is you're running from." He said and I gave him a 'are you serious' look.

"What's your gain from this?" I found myself asking. He smirked and that was a sight to behold.

"Nothing." He said.

He couldn't be serious right? How could he just openly accept me into his pack when he barely knew me? I could be a spy for all he knew.

He was starting to make me think he was doing all this because he was a little immature.

"How can you trust me so easily? What if I'm a spy?" I asked. He laughed at that and propped his arms forward on the table.

"I wouldn't care actually. I don't think this little girl is capable of inflicting harm. You're so precious." He said eyes twinkling with delight.

>>>>>>>>>

Hey lovelies.

Whom do you prefer, Axel or Miles? Let me know in the comments.

Pls vote. Love you all, bye

4.New Home

A xel's POV

We searched round the house but we didn't see Alyssa. Bianca searched her room and discovered that most of her things were gone.

She left.

I didn't know how to feel about that. I thought I hated Alyssa so much but not seeing her here anymore made me realize something.

I missed her.

Only now had I started to realize how foolish I was over the past three years. Alyssa didn't do anything wrong. Her parents passing wasn't her fault. She never meant for them to die.

I felt a missing piece in me. I couldn't be myself anymore. Mason was furious with me and so was I with myself.

I knew she left because of me. Because I rejected her. How could I have done that to my mate? Only now was I starting to realize the amount of pain she must have felt.

Everyone in the pack house was moody for the rest of the day. No one talked to each other. I could see Alyssa's absence had made us realize just how much she meant to us.

"I miss her." Bianca confessed as we all gathered around the table for lunch.

"I wonder where she is, if she's alright. She must be so lonely and scared. I can't believe how we neglected her these past three years. She was a mourning child for crying out loud!" Mom exclaimed, basking in sorrow.

"I've had some of the pack warriors go out to find her. So you guys shouldn't worry much." Dad said.

In all I just kept quiet. I didn't tell anyone yet about her being my mate. That would transfer all the aggressions towards me.

Call me selfish or whatever but I didn't want any issues now as I'll soon be taking over the Alpha position.

If I told them I rejected my mate, wouldn't that make me a bad leader?

I got up abruptly and left the dinning room. I didn't have any appetite for food.

My mate was out there, probably being tortured or dead already. The thought of that made me whimper.

I'm just starting to realize something.

I loved Alyssa a lot

Alyssa's POV

Alpha Miles was nothing I ever imagined an Alpha to be.

I accepted the deal if you could even call it that and now he was showing me around the pack house and introducing me to everyone.

I learnt a lot about him in just one afternoon.

Apparently he was an orphan and had to take over the Alpha position at age 16 after his father died in a war. I felt really sad for him. His childhood was stripped from him but I could tell he was a wise and courageous leader.

He had a twin sister Mila and she was just as energetic and bubbly as he was. She looked like the feminine version of him and I could tell why they were twins.

We immediately became best friends in a matter of minutes as apparently we had a lot in common.

From our favourite food to our taste in music, we were alike. She also told me she paints which was really cool.

I also got to know later about the three guys I met at the river.

The black haired one who manhandled me was Seth the beta. He was a year older than Miles. He was the strictest of them all. He later apologized for the way he rough handled me and explained his distaste for rogues after all his mother was killed by one. I understood quickly and sympathize with him. We were cool in an instant.

The brown haired one was Greg the gamma and he just happened to be this reserved guy who apparently had issues with talking to people. I knew it would need a lot of opening up before he and I could be close. He was the same age as Miles and Mila.

The blonde one Aiden was my age and very immature. He was a playboy according to Mila and all the maids in the house wouldn't stop flashing smiles and winking at him. But I liked him because he was charming and funny too. He made me laugh most of the time, making me forget my sorrows and worries. He was Miles and Mila's cousin.

Now I was in my new room which was fairly spacious and neat.

There was a twin bed, a wardrobe, a desk and a vanity. I had started unpacking my little belongins.

Miles insisted that I'd go shopping for more things tomorrow and I couldn't argue because he was very persistent. Mila offered to go with me and pick only the best outfits for me.

She was rather too ecstatic about squandering her brother's money.

I stared at the picture of my parents in my hands and a tear slid down my face.

Are they happy I made this decision? Are they happy I left our home?

A knock on the door snap me out of my daze and I quickly put the picture away, wiping my cheeks.

"Come in." I said. A head peaked in then Miles entered the room, smiling contagiously.

"Miles." I breathed.

"Hey. Came to inform you that dinner will be served soon." He said, eyes raking my small figure.

I blushed at his intense gaze and nodded.

"Okay."

"Tomorrow evening will be your induction into the pack." He said hands behind his back. Right now he was acting like a strict leader, all signs of playfulness forgotten.

I swallowed and nodded slowly.

This was a big deal.

To be inducted into another pack meant cutting off all your ties with your old pack. They'd feel it once it was done. Although you could always go back. But of course I wasn't planning to do that.

"Okay." I said and smiled. I was ready for this.

Miles and his pack members have been nothing but kind to me. Here I felt wanted. Here I felt happiness I haven't felt in three years.

"You should come out for dinner." He said and smiled at me before leaving.

I quickly put away the rest of my things and hurried after him.

I love my new home

>>>>>>>>>>>>>

Hey lovelies.

Hope you enjoyed this chap?

Pls vote. Love you all

Authoress out, peace

5.Inducted

Y ou're a beautiful person if you're reading
this____Alyssa'

POV

I got up early the next morning mainly because I couldn't sleep the entire night. I've been tossing and turning around on the bed. My tummy hurts really bad and I didn't know what was wrong with me.

I went into the bathroom and took a short shower. I was feeling a bit queasy and had light headache.

Whatever was wrong with me?

I towel dried my body and hair. I wore a yellow shirt and a pair of black jeans.

I put my long brown hair in a low ponytail and slid on my black sandals before walking out.

I was hearing voices from the kitchen as I walked there.

"Good morning pretty!" Aiden yelled on seeing me. Mila pulled me in for a hug and I hugged her back smiling.

What was with all the enthusiasm today?

Miles smiled at me as I approached the kitchen island.

"Good morning." I said.

"Morning sunshine. Did you have a good sleep?" He said while I blushed.

Why was he so sweet to me when he barely knew me?

"Huh...it was fine." I said slightly embarrassed because everyone was now looking at us.

I turned to Mila who was snickering.

"Good morning." I said to both Seth and Greg who were sitting opposite me.

"Morning." Seth replied sending me a small smile. Greg just nodded slightly and left the kitchen.

What was his problem anyway?

"Don't mind Gregory. He'll come around eventually." Seth said and I nodded.

The maid served me pancakes which was my all time favourite but looking at it now, I just felt like puking.

Not because it looked bad or anything but the smell of it made me feel more queasy.

"Excuse me. I'll be right back." I said and ran into my bathroom before I'd puke on the floor.

Crouching next to the toilet, I puked everything I hadn't even eaten.

I rinsed my mouth and flushed the toilet after. What was wrong with me? I don't normally get morning sickness like this.

Someone knocked on the bathroom's door and I opened it.

Mila was standing there with a worried look.

"Are you feeling okay?" She asked and I shook my head truthfully. I wasn't feeling okay and I wanted to know the cause of it.

She reached for my forehead to check my temperature and frowned.

"You're burning up. You should see the doctor." She suggested and I nodded.

I didn't have the strength to argue plus I don't normally get sick so I wanted to know if whatever was happening to me was serious.

"Let's go back to the kitchen. You have to eat first."

When we got to the kitchen everyone was looking at me worriedly. Why did they care so much? They knew me only just yesterday. My heart swelled at this.

I couldn't eat the pancakes as it'll make me just want to vomit so I settled for cereals.

After breakfast, Mila said we were going shopping and after that the Pack's doctor would be coming to check up on me.

We bought a lot of clothes, bags and shoes. Things I'd never use in a long time. I declined most of them but Mila was having none of it. She was the most tenacious girl I'd met.

After our shopping appointment, we went back home. Just as Mila said, there was a pack doctor there to see me.

He was an old man in his late sixties maybe. He had bald grey hair and a really short stature.

He was very kind and polite and introduced himself as Doctor Wills.

He asked me how I've been feeling for the past few days and I told him.

Fatigued, stressed, queasy...

"I'll be back with the test results tomorrow." He told me politely and I nodded. He left the room while I stood up from my bed.

I went to the bathroom to shower. Miles told me to come out for lunch when Dr Wills was done and after that would be the induction ceremony.

I was really nervous about that. I put on a black shirt and blue jeans. I curled the lower half of my hair and placed it in a high ponytail.

Sliding on my sandals, I left the room and went for lunch.

>>>>>>>>>>>>>

I was really nervous standing before the crowd as Miles was giving a speech that I totally zoned out on.

"So we will all welcome Alyssa Megara Brown to our pack." Miles said and turned to me. I raised an eyebrow at him and silently cursed myself for not paying attention.

A teenage boy ran towards us handing Miles a very sharp pocket knife. What did he need that for?

Miles suddenly cut his left palm with it and I widened my eyes.

He lightly smiled at me before stretching his hands to take mine. I gave him mine and he cut my palm open, shaking it after so that our bloods were now mixing.

"The process is now complete! Please all welcome Alyssa to our pack!" He addressed the crowd and everyone cheered.

>>>>>>>>>>>>>

I fluttered my eyes open and let out a yawn as I sat up on the bed. I was feeling really tired though I just woke up. The morning sickness was back again and now I was in the toilet throwing up what I haven't even eaten yet.

I flushed the toilet and rinsed my face staring at my reflection.

My face looked flushed seeing as I just awoke. I took a quick bath and put on a red sundress with black poka dots.

I let my hair down today as I couldn't fuss with it. I didn't have that strength.

I looked up at the wall clock and my mouth fell open.

12:15pm?

How long did I sleep for?

I went down to the kitchen and saw everyone gathered for brunch.

They were all talking loudly and laughing not noticing my presence.

I coughed awkwardly so they'd see me and they all paused, all staring at me.

"H..hi guys." I said waving awkwardly.

"Sleeping beauty's awake!" Aiden yelled. Mila rushed to hug me.

"Hey Aly." Miles said smiling, cutting me completely off guard.

He called me Aly. That's what my mom used to call me. I immediately blushed seeing how intensely he was staring at me.

"Come join us." Seth said and I nodded shyly before seating on the empty stool beside George who just continued eating without saying a word to me. But I didn't mind cos I was already getting used to it.

It was embarrassing seeing them all here together knowing I slept in.

Through brunch I could notice them exchanging looks with themselves. I didn't know what they meant by that I just continued eating silently.

After a few minutes, Mila suddenly stood up her stool falling back at the impact.

"Alright I don't care anymore. It's her right to know so she should." She said talking to no one in particular. I gave her a look before staring at everyone else.

Miles was giving her a worried look that read 'don't say anything'

Seth looked indifferent.

Aiden looked excited and George just kept eating, not really bothering about whatever Mila was saying.

Wait she? Was she talking about me? I was the only she here besides her. What did I have to know?

"Mila don't." Miles said.

"W... what's that?" I asked turning to Miles. He pursed his lips still looking at Mila.

"Doc Wills was here earlier." She said. "You're pregnant." She finished and my eyes widened.

"What?"

I was pregnant?! But how did that even happen?!

>>>>>>>>>>>

Hey lovelies

Sorry for the cliffhanger

Hope you guys enjoyed this chap. Pls vote and comment. Love you all

6.All Pink

Y ou're a beautiful person if you're reading this.__________________
________________________________Axel's POV

Things haven't been the same since Alyssa's disappearance. The search party wasn't able to find her since and they had all given up.

Everyone became quiet and only said a few words to each other. The pack house had become really gloomy.

I had taken over the Alpha position from my father and was doing a great job so far. I became this cold and strict Alpha simply because of the grieve of loosing my mate. Each passing day I felt that longing in my heart to see her. I was in an internal battle with my wolf.

He urged me everyday to go look for our mate but I just couldn't. As much as I wanted to find Alyssa, I couldn't neglect my Alpha duties. So I hired Manuel a secret agent to find my mate.

Alyssa's POV

It's been four months since I found out about my pregnancy. Everyone was treating me with so much love and care and for once again in my life, I started to feel loved.

I realized that I was carrying my mates baby. I didn't know how to feel about that after all he rejected me so I decided to raise my child alone and not let Axel know about him. I didn't want him to reject my baby too.

The others agreed with me. They were all very happy about the fact that a baby would be joining the family. Even Greg started opening up to me.

One time he bought me a baby blanket and these were his exact words.

"I went shopping for my blazers and just saw this blanket. I thought it'll be very nice for your baby so I bought it."

That was the most words Greg had ever spoken to me and I felt really overwhelmed.

Miles got really overprotective. He wouldn't let me do stuff and put me on bed rest for an entire day. I felt like a sick woman with the way he treated me.

I just wanted to snap at him and tell him that I was only pregnant not sick but I knew he was only looking out for my baby and I and that would hurt his feelings so I put up with him.

Mila on the other hand took it as her priority to make the baby room which was just next to mine. I wanted to refuse and say it's alright for my baby to live in my room but she blatantly refused.

She claimed that the baby had to have a room of his own so it'll feel independent even at a very young age. I didn't understand her logic but I couldn't argue either so I just obliged.

Presently we just had breakfast and we were both heading out to go baby shopping.

At the mall Mila kept picking out pink things and baby girl dresses.

"How are you sure the baby's gonna be a girl?" I asked her as I took out a blue diaper bag.

"Because I prayed so." She simply shrugged stuffing the cart with the things she was holding. "And how are you sure it'll be a boy?" She said eying the blue diaper bag I was holding.

"Oh. You can call it mother instincts." I said rubbing on my small baby bump.

She snorted and pushed the cart.

At the counter, the cashier looked at us like we were insane. I couldn't blame her though. Mila had outdid herself by stuffing two carts with baby toys and clothes. All pink.

I didn't bother to argue with her cos that'll just be a waste of breath and energy.

After the cashier packed everything, we had to phone Aiden and Greg to come help us out.

"Our little princess is gonna be the cutest." Aiden said once we were home going through the things we bought.

"Yeah, finally someone agrees with me that the baby's gonna be a girl." Mila said as she fist bumped Aiden.

"I want it to be a boy." Greg said making us turn our heads to him. He gave us a look that said 'what?' and shrugged. I smiled lightly. I liked this side of Greg.

"Actually it's gonna be a girl." Seth said suddenly at the door and we all turned to him. He was working with Miles in the office when did he get here?

"The room looks nice." He said observing the huge white crib at a corner of the room.

"It's not even near finished. Once we confirm the gender of the baby which actually isn't necessary as the baby's gonna be a girl, I'm going to paint this room pink." Mila said looking around dreamingly.

"I agree""I disagree"

Aiden and Greg said simultaneously and we all burst out laughing.

The next day was my ultrasound. Doc Wills smiled at me warmly as he rubbed the cold liquid over my tummy.

He placed the device on my belly and pointed to the black screen.

"Take a look at this Alyssa. Your baby is very healthy." He said smiling. I felt my heart swell with happiness as I looked at the blurry picture of my baby. It was so tiny. Something so precious was living inside of me.

Miles was beside me also looking into the screen smiling.

"What's the gender?" He asked.

"Uhm let's see..." Doc Wills said, running the device on my stomach.

"It's a boy." He said.

"That's marvellous." Miles said happily.

I'm going to have a little boy. A little prince. I smiled at that thought. My poor baby though. He's going to grow up without a father. A tear slid down my face at that thought.

Miles rubbed my arm and smiled at me encouragingly. I wiped my tears and smiled back.

Mila and Aiden were dumbfounded when we told them about the baby being a boy. Miles mocked them and Greg was happy.

Seth didn't mind anymore. He was just happy the baby was healthy.

We had to take out all the baby girl's things Mila bought and replace them with boy's things.

Mila, Aiden and I painted the room baby blue and we made little designs on the wall with white paint. The others also helped out and we all dipped our hands in the white paint and placed it on the wall making beautiful hand prints.

It was so much fun. There was so much love and happiness.

By evening time, we were done with the room. It looked so beautiful. Blue themed and special.

We were now having dinner and laughing over random jokes Aiden was making. I suddenly felt a sharp pain on my abdomen and cried out.

Everyone turned to me and Miles was beside me the next second.

"Are you alright?" He asked worriedly.

"No....my belly. It..it hurts." I said and felt the pain again. I stood up from the stool and held unto Miles scrunching my face in pain.

"We need to get her to the hospital. Seth get the car!" Was the last I heard before I totally blacked out.

>>>>>>>>>>>

Hey lovelies

Whose POV do you like better, Alyssa's or Axel's? Pls let me know in the comments.

Pls vote. Love you all, bye.

7.Baby names

Allysa's POV

I squinted my eyes as I tried to adjust to the bright light in the white hospital room. I could hear hushed voices whispering.

I fully opened my eyes and turned my head to the side to see Miles, Mila and Seth sitting on a couch by the corner of the large room.

I sat up slowly and they finally seemed to notice I was awake as they all rushed towards me.

"Ly, you're awake!" Mila said rearranging the pillow supporting my back.

"Hm." I only muttered. I was feeling pain coming from my lower abdomen. I noticed my baby bump was gone. I gave birth already?

"Are you okay? Do you hurt any-"

"Where's my baby?" I asked cutting Miles off.

"Oh, don't worry Ly. Your baby is very safe. He was born a few weeks earlier so the doctor put him in an incubator." Mila said and I calmed down.

A werewolf was supposed to stay a minimum of five months before it's born but my baby was born prematurely now he was in an incubator.

I kind of felt at fault for this. I wanted to meet my baby already.

"He's so cute Ly. He's got your pretty brown orbs and button nose." Mila said making me giggle lightly.

"I wanna see him." I said looking between Mila and Miles.

"Okay but we first have to take the doctor's permission." Miles said abruptly. I groaned in frustration. That would take forever. I just wanted to see my baby already.

"I'll go get him." Seth said flashing me a smile. I smiled back at him as he left.

"You didn't answer the previous question Aly. Are you in pain anywhere?" Miles asked and I shook my head not wanting him to worry.

Just then a nurse came in to check my vitals.

"You'll need to rest to regain your strength after all you just went through an operation." She said as she adjusted the drip.

"Operation?" I asked surprised. I went through an operation? It's no wonder I felt so weak.

"Yeah you had to undergo a CS operation as the baby would have died otherwise. He had to be born immediately due to certain complications during your pregnancy." The nurse explained and I just nodded.

Miles was looking at me as if to comfort me and I smiled lightly at him. I couldn't believe my baby was put at risk, all because of me.

Just then the doctor came in with Seth. He started ranting about how I shouldn't overstress myself and be in bed rest before he finally released me to go see my son.

He was the cutest little being I'd ever seen. He had my brown eyes like Mila said. Little patches of blonde hair were on his head and I knew he was going to be blonde like his father.

He was only wearing a diaper, wriggling nonstop in the incubator. I touched his tiny legs through the only available hole on the incubator. He started crying and I did the same.

I couldn't believe I gave birth to this little ball of sunshine. A wave of happiness and pride washed over me as I continued staring at my baby.

I already loved him so much and I vowed right then to always protect my son. I would keep him away from his father forever if that meant my baby could be safe and happy.

A week later, my baby and I were discharged along with a load of medics and vitamins for both of us respectively.

I didn't care that I had to take those bitter drugs, I only felt bad for my poor son who also had to take them.

I still hadn't decided a name for him yet and the guys took it has their job to name him.

"Let's just name him Milan. I'm telling you he'll thank me when he grows up." Mila said one morning while we were all having breakfast.

"Haha. I know you want him to be called Milan simply because it sounds like your name. I have a much better idea. We should name him Auden." Aiden said grinning.

"As if." Mila scoffed.

I looked between them and laughed.

"No. We should call him Arnest. I've always loved that name." Seth said rubbing his chin thoughtfully.

"Does that even have a meaning?" Mila said and Seth rolled his eyes.

"Of course it does." He said.

"What about Rolland?" Greg said meekly and we all burst out laughing.

He looked embarrassed and scratched his head.

"What's so funny?" He asked making us laugh even harder.

"You're just too innocent for the world Greg Greg." Mila said choking on her laughter.

"Don't call me that." Greg said frowning slightly.

"What's your suggestion Miles?" I asked changing the topic.

Miles was cut off guard as he cleared his throat.

"Uhm.... I....we should call him....uhm.... what about you? What do you wanna call him?" He suddenly diverted the question to me.

"I think Kian is a beautiful name." I said smiling.

"Wow. Mother knows best indeed! That's a nice name Ly." Mila said smiling contagiously.

"That wraps up the naming chapter then. Our little prince is therefore named Kian." Seth said.

"But is he going to have your last name?" Greg suddenly asked.

"As much as I don't like it, it'll be only right to give him his father's last name." I said.

"You're right girl." Mila said.

"Kian Rolland Braun." I said and Greg looked at me surprised.

"His middle name is gonna be Rolland?" He asked.

"Yeah, it's a lovely name." I replied and smiled at him.

Five Years Later

"Stop running now! I mean it little man, if you don't stop, you're going to be in big trouble once I catch you." I said running after my son Kian. He was just too energetic and hyper.

I was already feeling drained but he on the other hand seemed to have all the energy in the world.

"No mommy. I wanna play some more!" He yelled as he continued running.

We were in the living room and he was running around the sofas with me circling him.

I had to put him to bed as it was late already but he decided it was his mission to make my life harder tonight.

I stopped circling him and stood, arms akimbo.

"Alright listen up little guy. If you don't get here right this minute, I'm gonna-" I couldn't complete my sentence as Miles came behind Kian and picked him up.

"Alpha!" Kian squealed as Miles started tickling him. I smiled as I watched them both. They were so cute.

"Giving mommy a hard time? Is that what good boys should be doing?" Miles said as he seated Kian on the head of a couch and held him.

Kian shook his head cutely and I smiled.

"So what's the right thing to do?" Miles asked as he watched him strictly. It was always nice to see Miles acting like he was Kian's biological father. They loved each other so much.

"Say sorry to mommy and go to bed like a good boy." Kian said as Miles placed a kiss on his forehead before putting him down.

Kian ran to me and hugged my legs as he was still too short.

I smiled warmly and ruffled his hair.

"Sorry mama." He said and I picked him up. He immediately buried his face in my neck.

I walked towards Miles and smiled at him as I rocked Kian gently.

"How was the meeting with the Cross moon pack?" I asked and he sighed as he placed both hands in each of his pockets.

"We finally came to an agreement but it seems the war is still a possibility as Alpha Lawrence is so full of hatred." He said and patted Kian's head. He had already fallen asleep.

"You should go get some rest now. We'll talk more about it tomorrow." He said then touched my cheeks before leaving.

I went to Kian's room to put him to bed. For the past five years, Miles had been nothing but caring and affectionate. Those things I couldn't receive from my mate for the longest of time.

I knew he had feelings for me but I didn't want to acknowledge it because his mate was somewhere out there. If we end up becoming a family and he eventually finds his mate, what happens then?

One rejection is enough for me. I didn't want a mate to reject me again that's why I've been trying my best not to fall for him.

It's a good thing I had Kian. He was a very good distraction for me. I also had Nala. My wolf whom I got only a few months after I had Kian.

I was so wrong about her. She loved me so much and sympathized with me for what our mate did to us. She also agreed with me that I should never let our pup know about our mate.

It was just for the best.

As I successfully tucked Kian into his bed, I walked out of the room and closed the door.

I turned towards my own room's door but suddenly heard a loud crashing sound downstairs.

What was that?

I went downstairs and looked around and screamed when I saw a shadow by the window.

>>>>>>>>>>>

Hey lovely readers

I'm so sorry for the long awaited update. I hope you enjoyed this chapter.

Pls leave your thoughts in the comments and vote pls.

Love you all, bye

8.Big bad Alpha

You're a beautiful person if you're reading this_______________________________________Alyssa'
POV

I went downstairs and looked around and screamed when I saw a shadow by the window.

The shadow disappeared as the lights went on.

"What happened Aly?! Are you alright?" Miles was suddenly standing front of me, examining me with worried eyes.

I was still in a trance from the shock I just got.

"Th...there was someone h..here." I breathed and gulped as I turned back towards the window.

It was slightly opened proving that someone had indeed come in through the window.

"Shit. Who could it be?" Seth who I hadn't noticed was there before muttered as he looked outside the window then shut it.

"I can smell mint leaves. The intruder must be into herbs." Miles said.

"It could be a rogue. I'll go check with the pack warriors." Seth said and exited the house.

"Are you okay?" Miles rested his hands on my shoulder as I shaked slightly.

"What would this person want? How did he even get pass the pack's border with all the warriors stationed there. Miles I'm really scared for my son. Someone could be out for him for all we know." I said anxiously and Miles pulled me into him, holding me gently.

"Nothings gonna happen to you or Kian. Not while I'm still here. You have nothing to fear or worry about." He said, rubbing soothing circles on the small of my back.

"Just trust me."

Axel's POV

I hit the last ball fiercely and ran a hand through my blonde locks as I watched the small volleyball run and fall into the hole.

"Voila! I knew none could defeat you. You're the Alpha after all." Dad said a little too excited.

"C'mon dad, you know I'm only good simply because I learnt from the best.". I said as I picked my water bottle and gulped down it's content.

"I heard there's a supposed war between the Cross moon pack and Blue stone pack?" Dad said bringing me a white towel.

"So I heard. Alpha Lawrence is a blood thirsty man and I always thought Alpha Miles was too young when he took the Alpha title." I replied and poured the remaining water from my bottle over my head.

"He doesn't stand a chance against Alpha Lawrence." I said wiping my face with the white towel.

"You're right son and this could actually be an opportunity for you." Dad said eyes glistening with delight.

"How do you mean?" I asked.

He took a sit opposite me and clasped his hands.

"Don't you get son? What I mean is, you should join forces with Alpha Miles. Support him in the war. That way we'll have an Ally. I heard he leads a victorious Army. Imagine our packs coming together, how strong we will be." Dad said, constantly demonstrating with his hands to give more effect to his words.

"You're right Dad. That is actually very thoughtful of you." I smiled at him. "I'll contact Alpha Miles now." I finished and went to my office inside the pack house.

I punched in some numbers on my office phone and dialed it.

"Hello? Alpha Miles. Can you hear me?" I said.

'Yes. Who am I speaking with?" I heard the deep voice on the other end.

I didn't know why I felt at peace while making this phone call. It was like someone special was near.

"This is Alpha Axel of blue moon pack. I heard about the supposed war between your pack and cross moon pack. How would you like to strike a deal with me?" I asked one hand in my pocket.

"And what's this deal about?" He asked curtly.

"How about you invite me to your pack so we can talk in person about this?" I asked and he hummed.

"How about tomorrow by noon?" He asked.

"Yeah that would do. I'll look forward to meeting you then Alpha Miles." I said and ended the call.

The following day I got dressed and set to leave for Blue moon pack with Austin and Jason.

The trip took three hours and I was exhausted by the time we reached. The beta Seth and gamma Gregory welcomed us to the pack and led us to the pack house.

Mason was getting restless from the minute we entered the pack house but I couldn't understand why and I really didn't have the strength to deal with him.

I met Alpha Miles in his office and I couldn't help but pick a peculiar scent. A scent that has been inscribed in my memory for so long.

'Mate, mate. Our mate is near.' Mason yelled in my head.

That's why he's been so restless. My mate was here?

I got cut from my trance by Alpha Miles who cleared his throat.

"So what's the deal about Alpha Axel?" He asked.

"How many people live in this house?" I suddenly asked catching him off guard.

Everyone looked at me confused at my question.

"Why would you want to know that?" Alpha Miles said and and I took a deep breath trying to control my raging wolf. He was so eager to find our mate.

"Listen I don't have time to explain just answer me please." I said.

"Only my family live here. We have no employees whatsoever." Alpha Miles said and I frowned.

If he was telling the truth why was my mates scent so strong here? Why could not just me but also mason feel her so close?

"Okay. Let's just get on with the meeting." I said defeated. Maybe my mate wasn't here after all and it was all a mistake.

I explained the terms and everything about the deal and he signed the agreement.

We were already rounding up when a little boy with blonde hair ran into the room.

I was mesmerized by his resemblance to me as a little boy. He ran towards Alpha Miles and hugged his legs.

"Mommy's not back... Lily is tired of playing.... I'm getting hungry." The little boy kept mumbling to Alpha Miles. I didn't know why but I felt a pang of jealousy watching them both. I felt like that kid should be hugging me not him.

"I'm sorry Alpha Axel. I'll have to leave you and my beta to the rest as I have to tend to this little guy." He said to me and I nodded lightly.

The kid smiled at me flashing me his cute dimples. His deep brown orbs reminded me of my mates and I couldn't help but want to touch him.

They left the room and the beta Seth and I rounded up quickly.

"Thank you for your time Alpha Axel." Beta Seth said to me while seeing me off.

"It was nothing. I look forward to meeting again." I said.

I walked to my car parked outside the house. My phone started ringing and I told Austin and Jason to get in the car.

I took my phone from my pocket and saw it was Mom calling.

I was about to answer when someone crashed into me.

"What the fuck!" I turned around to see the little boy from earlier and a little girl beside him.

"You're cursing. Mommy says it's bad to curse." He said and the little girl suddenly started crying.

"Hey what's going on? Why are you crying suddenly?" I asked and I squatted to their level and patted the girls cheek to try soothe her.

"You're cursing at my brother. Bad Alpha, bad." She said crying. How did she know I was an Alpha though? I guess even pups could sense an Alpha's aura.

"You made my sister cry!" The boy suddenly yelled at me and hit me on my torso.

I couldn't believe how a kid's hit could hurt so much.

"Hey I'm sorry okay?" I said trying to contain the pain in my torso.

"Now you have to compensate Lily. Big bad Alpha." The boy said to me and I tried to hide my smile.

The kid was so cute trying to protect his little sister.

"Alright what do you want then?" I asked the little girl who had stopped crying.

"Will you come to my party tomorrow." She said.

"Sure." I replied without thinking twice and she smiled broadly.

I waved goodbye to the kids and turned towards my car when something or someone rather caught my attention.

Hey sweeties. Your authoress is so sorry to have kept you all waiting for a long time.

Happy new year

Hope you enjoyed this chapter. Love you all

9.He's my mate

You're a beautiful person if you're reading this

POV

I waved goodbye to the kids and turned towards my car when something or someone rather caught my attention.

I chuckled lightly at the sight before me.

A woman was running from across the street towards my direction, completely dressed like a clown.

"Mama!" The little girl I just spoke with yelled, giggling and jumping as the woman approached her.

I smiled as I watched the woman carry her daughter showering her with kisses. I suddenly felt an unusual emotion.

If Alyssa had never left, no scratch that. If I hadn't rejected her, maybe we would have been a happy family by now, probably had pups of our own.

I was suddenly cut from my thoughts when I felt a small hand on mine.

It was the little boy.

"Aunt Mila's talking to you, aren't you gonna reply her?" He said raising his eyebrow at me.

He was so cute...

"My cookie here said she invited you to her birthday, Alpha. So we're expecting you yeah?" The woman who was supposedly Aunt Mila said and I nodded.

"Your daughter managed to win my heart." I said and patted the little boy's head before turning to my car.

"What the hell man, we've been waiting for ages!" Austin yelled the minute I got into the car.

"I was caught up with two little fellas." I said and smiled at the memory of the adorable kids I just encountered.

"What's that bro, you're smiling!" Jason exclaimed and I glared at him through the rearview mirror.

He was at the back seat and Austin was at the passengers seat.

I started the engine while Austin kept staring at me.

"At this rate I'd get us into an accident. Why do you keep staring at me?" I asked five minutes into the drive and Austin was still staring.

"I never thought you like kids." He shrugged and finally looked away.

"Well I guess I do now." I smiled lightly.

Alyssa's POV

"Twenty eight, twenty nine and thirty!" Kian yelled and jumped, clapping his hands in happiness.

I smiled widely as I watched my son revel in his small victory.

I had been teaching him to count from 1-30 and before now he could only get to 23.

"Alright my prince, you're free to rejoice but the entire work isn't done yet okay?" I said and he came to sit on my lap.

I placed him comfortably on my lap and he wrapped his hands around my neck.

He gave me a kiss on my left cheek and I smiled at him.

"Hmm, what was that for?" I asked as he grinned.

"For being the best mommy!" He said and hugged me.

"Oh my son is so sweet." I said as I hugged him tightly while kissing his head.

"Awwn such a sweet moment, I'm jealous." Aiden was suddenly in the living room pouting.

I laughed at his childishness as I pulled apart from Kian.

"Uncle Aiden!" Kian squealed and jumped off my body, running towards Aiden.

"How are you doing little man?" Aiden asked ruffling his hair.

"I'm great!"

"It's Lily's party today, what gift have you gotten her?" Aiden asked Kian.

"It's supposed to be a surprise!" Kian said. Just then Mila, Anthony and Lily walked in.

Mila found her mate, Anthony a few months after Kian was born. They had Lily when Kian turned one.

Their chemistry was so strong and amazing. Anthony moved to the pack house, expanding the family.

Greg also found his mate Sara a few months ago. It was a new growth on him because he became more outgoing. They loved eachother dearly and were expecting a baby soon.

"Lily!"

"Kian!"

Both kids ran to hug each other.

How they were both so close and loved eachother like real siblings was really heartwarming.

"Oh come on. You both saw each other yesterday not last year." Aiden said dramatically and everyone laughed.

"Happy birthday Lily. I made you a card!" Kian said and ran to the centre table where I was teaching him and picked up the pink cardboard he made Miles buy a couple days ago.

"It's for me?" Lily asked as Kian gave her the cardboard.

"I wrote you a birthday wish and how much I love you." Kian said and everyone awwed at that.

"Alright time for the cake!" Aiden yelled.

"We'll have the cake during the party Aid. Why don't you come help with the decorations instead?" Mila said as she pulled Aiden away.

I also went to help with the preparations for the party.

I, Mila and Sara were in charge of the catering.

Aiden, Greg and Anthony were in charge of the decorations and setting up the ball room for the party.

While Miles and Seth were in charge of the guest lists and buying whatever we needed.

By noon, the whole party was set and Aiden had started blasting some music. The guests also started arriving.

"Ly, at this rate I just really wanna kick some people's ass. It's a kid's party not a stripper's club!" Mila grunted while we were in the kitchen finishing up with the cake.

I laughed at that and looked over at Sara who was doing the same.

"But she's right yunno. Have you seen Mirabelle in there? She's totally dressed like a whore. I really don't want my Greg looking at her." Sara said rubbing on her baby bump.

"Exactly my point! Anthony wouldn't stop glancing at her every three seconds and anytime I catch him staring I make sure to pinch him real hard!" Mila fused.

"It's alright you guys. You know both your mates loves you dearly and wouldn't dare to cheat." I comforted.

Just then Miles came in.

"Alpha Axel is here and said you invited him, Mila."

"Oh Lily did actually." Mila said smiling.

Alpha Axel? But there was only one Alpha Axel

I felt my hands shaking.

Axel was here? But how? And why?

"Are you okay Aly?" Miles was immediately by my side.

"Alp....Alpha Alex. He...he...he's my mate." I breathed shakily.

"What?!" Both Mila and Sara said at the same time.

Miles was silent but I could see lot of emotions on his face.

Anger, annoyance and Jealousy?

"That explains why he made the contract. He probably found out you lived here. It also explains why he was suddenly curious about who lived here. That fucking bastard!

I won't let him take you away from me Alyssa. That's never going to happen." Miles said and I shivered at the death look in his eyes. I have never seen him this angry.

>>>>>>>>>>>>

Hey guys!!!

How have you all been? So sorry for the unexpected haitus

Had serious exams to prepare for but don't worry, I'm not gonna ghost out on you guys again

Hope you all enjoyed this chapter, do well to leave your thoughts on the comment section and vote please

Love you all!!!

10.The birthday party

You're a beautiful person if you're reading this____

POV

I was already at the kid's party, sitting and observing. It was filled were-wolves from different packs. I could recognize some Alphas I have once made deals with and even some I just loathed.

A lady approached me smiling flirtatiously. She was wearing skimpy and really tight clothing and her overcaked make up just made me want to throw up.

Mason was trying to take over and rip this woman into shreds.

"Alpha Alex!" She squealed and sat next to me.

"Didn't expect to see you here today but then again Alpha Miles did invite Alphas from all round the country to celebrate his niece! By the way you look so handsome as usual! Can I just-"

"Get lost." I said abruptly and she stared at me surprised.

"Oh but I wasn't finished yet-"

"You don't want me repeating myself. It wouldn't end well for either of us."
I said again.

She stood up and left angrily but I didn't fucking care.

I had more issues at hand. Like Mason for example wasn't exactly still. He
was being totally restless.

I could understand why he was feeling that way but it made no sense. Our
mate was near. I could feel her and he could too.

Just then the little boy and girl approached me.

"You came!" The little girl said while the boy smiled.

"Yes princess. Tell me what's your name?"

"Lily! And he's Kian." She replied smiling cutely.

"So Lily how old are you today?" I asked touching her chubby cheeks.

She looked at me thoughtfully then pointed both pinky fingers to me.

"Two?" I grinned knowing she miscounted.

"She's four! Lily didn't I tell you, you're supposed to show four fingers. Just
like this." Kian said showing her both his pinkys and ring fingers.

"Oh." Lily said, sad at the mistake she had made.

"It's alright Lily. You don't have to be sad. Everyone makes mistakes." I said
trying to make her happy again. Then I took the plastic bag beside me and
brought out the gift box covered in pink wrapper.

"It's for me?" Lily asked and I smiled.

"Don't see any other princess here whose birthday is today." I said and she
grinned.

She took the box admiring it.

"Thank you Alpha." She said and I patted her hair, slightly shifting her tiara.

I fixed it properly and touched her chubby cheeks, smiling.

"Someone is in love with my daughter." I looked up to see Mila looking better in a blue dress than yesterday when she was dressed as a clown.

"Mommy, I got a gift." Lily said showing her mom the pink box.

"This is nice. Thank you Alpha." Mila said and I nodded.

"We're about to cut the cake and sing for Lily. Come on front." Mila said, taking the kids away and I followed shortly behind them.

With each step I took to the front, Mason kept becoming restless. My mate's scent was getting stronger. I didn't understand what was happening.

If my mate was really around why couldn't I see her? The ball room was big and filled with people but it should have been easier to see her right? Afterall she's my mate. We shared a bond. Though I rejected her, she never accepted it so our bond wasn't broken yet.

She could also feel my presence right? Was she hiding from me then? Where was she?

I changed my motive from following Mila to finding my mate. I left the ballroom and came to the hallway. I knew what I was about to do was wrong especially for an Alpha.

I shouldn't be venturing round someone's house but I was eager and desperate to find my mate. I followed her scent from where it seemed stronger.

It wasn't that evident in the ballroom because lots of people with different scents were in there but here in the hallway, I could smell her stronger.

I found a staircase and led my way up to it.

Getting to the very last step, I came face to face with Alpha Miles.

He looked angry and annoyed on seeing me. Did he realise I was patrolling round his house?

"Hi Alpha Miles. Didn't see you again after you left the ballroom." I said smiling cooly.

"I wasn't exactly free. I had things to take care of." He said. "But what are you doing here? You're supposed to be at the party." He asked.

"Oh yeah. I was just finding the restroom. Sorry for wandering." I lied smoothly and he nodded.

"Funny because there's a restroom in the ballroom." He said and walked down the stairs. I fisted my palm angry that he just had to ruin my plans.

I followed behind him like a lost puppy as we got to the ball room.

"Enjoy the party. I'll see you later." He said as he stopped at a door which I assumed was the restroom.

"Sure." I replied and he left.

I sighed and looked around.

Everyone was busy singing for the little princess. I left the ballroom again but this time went outside to the large compound.

If Alpha Miles wasn't an Alpha, I would have said he was a little too rich but then again who was I to judge when I was also guilty of the same crime?

I walked to the car park and leaned backwards on my car. I placed a hand over my eyes as I basked in the warmth of the sun.

"Everyone's inside." I looked down, surprised to see Kian.

"Hey champ. What you doing out here?" I asked ruffling his hair.

"Mommy made my hair. Don't ruin it!" He said aggressively.

"Sorry champ." I squatted to his level and held his hands.

"You really love your mommy much, hmm?" I said and he nodded.

"My mommy is the best! I love her absolutely much." He said and I smiled.

"Then shouldn't you be with your mommy right now?" I asked thoughtfully.

"But Mommy said to stay with Lily. Mommy has been in her room. She wouldn't even come out for Lily's party." He said sadly and pouted.

I patted his cheeks and carried him up placing him on the bonnet of my car.

"Tell me, where's your mommy? Maybe we can convince her to come out together, hmm?" I asked and his face brightened.

"Okay let's go inside!" He said and I put him down.

He pulled my wrist, dragging me along with him.

He was a little too excited to see his mom.

On getting inside, I noticed the party was already over and the guests had started leaving.

He was already taking me up the stairs when Alpha Miles stopped us.

"Where do you think you're going?"

>>>>>>>>>>>>

Sup lovelies

Hope you liked this chapter

Whoooo I'm getting the goosebumps

11.We'll find her soon

You're a beautiful person if you're reading this

POV

I was lying on my bed thinking about everything happening in my life.

After what Miles said in the kitchen, I knew for a fact that he was in love with me and would do anything to protect me.

So I asked him not to let Axel know about my presence in this pack and to keep Kian as far away from him as possible.

I had been in been in my room because I didn't want to encounter Axel by accident.

Now the party was over, I decided to leave to room, praying and begging the moon goddess to not let me see Axel once I got out there.

I walked briskly down the stairs and saw Mila and Lily.

"Hey girl." She said smiling, trying to ease my mood knowing I was still shaken up from seeing my mate.

"Hey. I'm really sorry I couldn't be out there for Lily's party." I said solemnly, caressing lily's chubby cheeks.

"It's alright dear. I understand you totally and there's really a no need to apologize. Besides you promised to celebrate Lily specially." She said and winked at me.

I smiled and took Lily from her arms.

"How about your favourite treat sweetie? Then we can go to an arcade with Kian sometime." I asked Lily and she nodded happily.

With that I took her to the kitchen to prepare her favourite treat.

Axel's POV

"See you next time then." I said shaking hands with Alpha Miles.

After he saw me by the stairs, I told him of Kian's request and he told me not to worry that Kian's mom wasn't feeling too well.

He then saw me off.

Something was strange about him but I couldn't just point a finger to what.

In my office back in my pack, I was going through some documents I received earlier today when I heard a knock on the door.

"Come in." I said not looking away from the stash of paperwork.

"Alpha. I got some information on Alyssa." Manuel said bowing slightly to show his respect. (In case you don't remember, Manuel was the secret spy Axel hired to find Alyssa)

"What did you get?" I asked immediately, putting away the paperwork.

"She lives in Blue stone pack Alpha." He said.

I knew she lived there. It just had to be. I felt uneasy anytime I visited that pack. But that information wasn't enough. I needed to know where exactly she was. How she was doing.

Wait she must have had to go through Alpha Miles before she could live there right? That means he must have some information about the whereabouts of my mate.

"Alright thank you Manuel, you may leave." I said and picked up my phone, dialing Alpha Miles' number.

I needed to find out where Alyssa was right away.

He picked up almost immediately.

"Hi. I know I left not too long ago but I have a question for you." I started.

"What's that?"

"Is there an Alyssa Megara Braun living in your pack?" I asked knowing he might likely not know who I was talking about but still hoping for something.

There was a bit of silence on the other end then he replied.

"I'm not sure who you're talking about, sorry."

I sighed in frustration.

"Can you search your pack's record for that person? It's really important I find her." I said.

"Last I remember, you signed a contract with me not with a member of my pack, so what do you need from this person?" He asked gruffly.

I didn't understand why he was acting that way. He was normally nice and calm but right now he was acting like me.

"She happened to be a runaway from my pack about five to six years ago. And I recently found out she lives in your pack. I need to talk to her." I said trying to control my already rising temper.

"Oh I'm not sure I have anyone like that in my pack. Every member of my pack was born here." He said and I slammed the phone angrily, breaking it into pieces.

I hit the table and ran a hand over my blonde locks. Why was I so unfortunate?

If Alyssa wasn't in Blue stone pack then where the fuck was she? Did Manuel get me wrong information then or was Alpha Miles lying to me?

I was so frustrated at these never ending questions with no answers.

The door flung open and in came my Mom, Dad and Bianca.

"What's going on?!" Dad asked as Mom rushed towards me.

"I need to find her! I'm so fucking tired of missing every detail!" I yelled angrily and stood up from my chair.

"Find who?" Mom asked.

"My mate, Alyssa. I need to find her." I replied.

"What?!" They all exclaimed and only then did I remember I never told them about Alyssa being my mate.

"Alyssa is your mate?" Bianca asked.

"Yes." I mumbled.

"Why did you never tell us then?" Mom asked.

"I rejected her, she left because I did that." I said solemnly.

"What?!" They all yelled again and I sighed.

"Why though? Why did you reject your mate?" Mom asked, tears welling up in her eyes.

"I was young and foolish Mom. I didn't realize the gravity of my actions until it was too late. I regret it every single day. I really do." I said.

"You should have told us son, then we would have worked harder towards finding her." Dad said and I sighed.

"I'm really sorry for not telling you guys. I was just ashamed of myself for rejecting her." I said and Mom hugged me.

"It's alright my son. We're going to find her soon." Mom said, rubbing my back while I hugged her tightly, trying to hold back my tears.

I really missed my mate.

Mason needed her.

I needed her

"I'll create a new search party and this time only with the best. We'll find her no matter what." Dad said and I smiled.

>>>>>>>>>>>

Hey lovelies

Hope you enjoyed this chapter, please vote and comment

12.She's here

You're a beautiful person if you're reading this____

POV

I placed the last spoon of pancake batter in the fry pan and Kian peered at me with watchful eyes.

"Mommy how long is it gonna take for this one to fry?" He asked curiously.

"A few seconds baby." I replied and flipped the pancake over.

"Did it also take a few seconds for those other ones to fry?" He asked again pointing to the tray of pancakes I made before.

I smiled at him as I took the pancake out of the pan and turned off the stove.

"Yes dear." I said, placing a plate of pancake before him.

"Something smells divine." I heard Miles deep voice as he entered the kitchen.

"Alpha!" Kian yelled in between munching on his pancakes.

"Hey champ. Happily eating?" Miles asked sitting beside Kian.

Kian nodded.

"Also want some?" I asked knowing fully well he might say no after all he doesn't eat pancakes.

"Yeah." He said surprising me.

I smiled at him and served him a plate of pancakes.

"Any work today?" I asked cleaning the utensils I used in cooking.

"I do have a meeting with Alpha Lawrence. He suddenly called for one. He probably heard of the alliance with our pack and Blue moon pack and now wants a peace treaty." He said.

"That's a good thing then, we should probably celebrate." I said smiling.

"Hmm hmm." Miles replied non chalantly.

He was probably still upset after finding out Axel was my mate.

"Aunt Alyssa!" Lily ran into the kitchen and hugged me tightly.

I dried my hands and carried her.

"Oh baby. A good morning to you too." I said and pecked her cheeks. Anthony entered the kitchen and we exchanged greetings.

"Alpha, the pack warriors have been assembled." He whispered to Miles but I heard him.

"Alright." Miles replied and Anthony nodded.

"Daddy!" Lily yelled and Anthony smiled and walked towards us.

"She's a little to excited today." Anthony said as Lily jumped into his embrace.

"And you're busy. Give her to her mother, let's leave." Miles said standing up.

"It's alright Anthony. I'll take her." I said and took Lily from him.

"Thanks a bunch Alyssa!" Anthony said and left with Miles.

I sighed as Lily smiled brightly at me, also bringing a smile to my face.

Miles was unhappy, I could sense it but there was nothing I could do about it.

"Mommy all done!" Kian yelled and got down from his high chair.

"That's good baby. Now let's get ready cos we're going to the park!" I announced and both kids squealed happily.

I informed Mila and Sara that I was taking the kids out and Aiden begged to tag along.

I couldn't refuse him after all I'd need a helping hand with both kids.

The kids kept singing all the way to the fun park and I couldn't stop smiling.

They got on all fun rides and played many games.

"I need to pee pee." Lily said while we were buying cotton candies.

"Oh Aiden can you take her to the kiddies restroom, I need to pay for these." I said and Aiden nodded and carried Lily.

"Mommy my candy!" Kian said reaching for the cotton candy on my hand.

"Here you go." I handed him one and payed to the vendor.

"Alright let's go to Uncle Aiden and Lily." I said as we headed towards the restrooms.

"Mommy it's Mario!" Kian yelled pointing to a Mario mascot.

He slipped his hand out of mine and ran towards the mascot.

"Kian!" I yelled and ran after him.

The place was suddenly crowded and I lost sight of Kian.

"Kian! Kian! Kian!" I kept yelling looking around for my baby boy.

Just then Aiden approached me holding Lily in his arms.

"What happened Alyssa?" He asked worriedly.

"Kian. He just ran off, I can't find him.." I said my voice cracking at the end.

I was already crying.

"Fuck! I'll look around. Stay here with Lily." He said and put Lily down.

"My poor baby." I cried as I kept looking around frantically, hoping my son would run back to me.

Axel's Pov

I told Dad about Manuel's report and the strong feeling of my mate's presence whenever I was at Blue stone pack.

He said I should go to Blue stone pack and confirm my suspicions.

I did as he said and now I was in Alpha Axel's office, sitting opposite him.

"Alpha Miles, with all due respect, you're mistaken because there's no Alyssa Megara Braun in this pack." He said clearly annoyed.

This only made me want to press on for more because he wouldn't be so worked up if for a fact Alyssa wasn't in this pack.

"It's very important I find her because she is my MATE." I said laying emphasis on the mate because I wanted him to understand how important it was to find her.

"Oh I didn't know you have a mate." He said indifferently.

"I did, not until she left." I replied.

"Or you mean not until you rejected her." He said bluntly and I raised a brow at him.

"Interesting, Alpha. How did you know that?" I asked and before he could reply, his beta and gamma barged in.

"Alpha! We just received news from Aiden that Kian went missing." The beta spoke and my eyes widened.

Kian was missing but how? For some reason I was really worried.

"What?!" Alpha Miles sprang up and rushed to his beta.

"What do you mean by that? Where are the others?" He asked frantically.

The Beta looked at me warily before replying.

"Aiden is still looking for him."

Alpha Miles nodded then turned to me.

"I'm sorry but my PUP is missing and I need to find him. You may return some other day when I'm free." He said and left with his Beta and Gamma.

Kian was his Pup? How did I never think of that? I never heard any information regarding Alpha Miles finding his mate so how?

I sighed as I suddenly had an evil thought.

I immediately started looking through the files and documents on the shelf in hope to find the Pack's record.

After ten minutes of futile searching, I finally found the file that had Pack's record written on it.

I smiled and I opened it and looked through the papers.

I went to five years back and my heart stopped as I came across a name that was forever etched on my memory.

My mate's.

She's here

>>>>>>>>>>>>Hello sweethearts

I'm reallyyyy sorry for the pretty late update.

I kind of abandoned this app for a while to focus on my school work. But I'm back now for you guys

So as an atonement for my sin I'm going to be doing a double update today

Enjoy guys!!!!

13.Kidnapped

A lyssa's Pov

The moon goddess probably wanted to punish me for keeping my mate from his Pup and that's why I was still here looking for my son.

"Aly!" I heard Miles voice and saw him, Seth, Greg and Anthony running towards us.

"Miles." I fell into his embrace and cried uncontrollably.

"My baby, my pup. He..he.."

"It's alright Aly. We're going to find him." Miles said and wiped my eyes.

He turned towards Anthony who was holding Lily and said.

"You take Alyssa and Lily home. Make sure they're all safe at home."

Anthony nodded and gestured for me to follow him.

"It's gonna be okay Alyssa. We'll find him, that's a given." Anthony sounded so sure.

Axel's Pov

I couldn't believe this. My mate was here in blue stone pack, I knew it!

But why did Alpha Miles lie to me then?

Whatever the reason, I didn't care. I was just happy to confirm that my mate was really here.

The address on her details said the pack house and I frowned.

She lived here all along but I never saw her even once? Come to think of it, I couldn't sense or smell her today.

Did she go out?

I put the files back together and left the office.

On my way outside the house, I bumped into Mila.

"Alpha Axel. Fancy seeing you here again." She said nervously making me wonder why.

"Oh yeah, I had a meeting with Alpha Miles." I said placing both hands in my pants' pockets.

"Really? I thought he had a meeting with Alpha Lawrence?" She asked.

"He happened to be leaving while I was coming in." I answered and she nodded.

"By the way. An Alyssa lives here right?" I asked and her eyes widened.

"What....huh no. I didn't know who that is!" She answered almost immediately.

I tilted my head and raised a brow at her.

She was obviously hiding something.

"Uhm....uhm...you should ask Alpha Miles about that." She said fidgeting.

"You live in this house so shouldn't you know?" I asked.

"Yes but I still think you should ask Alpha Miles." She said and ran off before I could say another word.

She's suspicious. It felt like they were hiding my mate, but why?

Did Alyssa realise I found her whereabouts and asked that she be hid? Then was she hiding from me?

Then again I wouldn't be surprised if she was actually hiding from me.

I was this close to finding her and at the same time not.

If my mate lived here, I was going to wait until she returned.

I sat in my car parked outside the compound, watching keenly in case my mate should come.

Alyssa's Pov

We arrived at the house and Anthony helped me out of the car.

I was much too distressed to notice anything.

We were walking towards the door when I heard an all too familiar voice call my name.

I looked back and my eyes widened as they fell upon none other than my mate.

He was standing by the gate looking as handsome as I could remember.

Those grey eyes I once fell in love with peered at me.

"Alyssa." He said, taking silent steps towards me.

"Axel." I breathed.

"It's Alpha!" Lily bounced up and down in her father's arms.

"Alyssa." Anthony held my hand and gave me a look that said go inside.

I looked back at Axel who was frowning at mine and Anthony's intertwined hands.

"Can I talk to him for a few minutes Anthony?" I asked with pleading eyes.

Nala was leaping with joy in my insides. She was meeting her mate for the first time.

"Okay but make it snappy. Alpha Miles would be happy if he found out about this." Anthony said and left.

"Alyssa I've been looking for you for so long." Axel said as he finally reached me.

I stepped back not knowing what to do or how to react.

He rejected me and now he was suddenly back telling me he had been looking for me, why though?

"Listen Aly." My heart skipped a beat

I felt my eyes tearing up.

All these emotions were too much for me. My pup was missing, I saw my mate after five years and I just didn't know what to do.

"I was really stupid back then for rejecting you. I had no idea what I was doing. Only after you left did I realise it. I've missed you greatly. Please come back to me Aly." He said, his voice filled with so many emotions.

"You rejected me." I finally spoke, the tears now spilling freely.

"I know and I'm truly sorry, please forgive me Aly. I'm really pathetic without you." He said and I could see he was on the verge of tears.

Just then Miles arrived. He looked between Axel and I and frowned.

"What are you still doing here Alpha Axel?" Miles asked.

"I'm here for my mate and I'm taking her with me." Axel said, his eyes full of anger.

"Alyssa isn't going anywhere. You rejected her so she's not your mate!" Miles yelled and I flinched.

"So you knew all along. You knew she was my mate yet you fucking hid her from me?!" Axel yelled back fuming.

"She doesn't need you anymore, you rejected her so leave!" Miles yelled again.

I was already tired at both of them yelling nonstop. My son was missing and that was the most important matiat hand.

"Can you both just shut up?!" I yelled and they both stopped and looked at me.

I walked towards Axel.

"Please leave Axel. I really don't need you here right now." Tears flowed down my cheeks as I watched his pained expression.

Nala whimpered totally disagreeing with me.

She was supposed to understand why I was doing this. But then again she wasn't there when my mate rejected me so I wouldn't expect her to understand.

"Aly please."

Just then my phone rang and I picked it immediately without checking the caller's ID.

'If you want your son alive and well, then you better do as you're told henceforth.'

The person on the other end said and I froze.

My baby has been kidnapped!

>>>>>>>>>>Hey sweet cheeks

I hope you enjoyed both chapters

Leave your answers in comments

Love you all

14.He's your son?

You're a beautiful person if you're reading this____

Pov

I had been in the car for over thirty minutes, patiently waiting for a sign of my mate.

A sleek black car finally pulled up at the gate and I unlocked my car ready to get out.

The car entered the compound and just before the gate could close, I walked in.

The car got parked at the garage and a man stepped out.

He failed to notice me and turned around to open the passenger's door and back door.

My heart stopped beating for a minute and Mason ran wild inside of me the moment Alyssa stepped out of the car.

My beautiful mate Alyssa

They walked towards the front door and before they could get in, I called Alyssa.

She looked at me with surprise and shock. I couldn't blame her though. She definitely wasn't expecting to see me here today.

The man beside her who was holding Lily, held Alyssa's hand and I felt rage.

She was my mate so why the fuck was he holding her?

I called out to her again and walked towards her.

She whispered my name and it did things to my insides.

Lily called out to me bouncing happily in the man's arms.

If we were in some other situation, I probably would have taken her in my arms and played with her but right now, I needed to focus on my mate.

The man held Alyssa's hand and I frowned at that.

This man was really pushing my buttons.

Alyssa told him she'd like to talk to me for a few minutes and he told her to make it snappy as Alpha Miles wouldn't be happy about this

What did Alpha Miles have to do in all of this? Why does she need permission to even talk to me? She is my fucking mate.

I covered the little distance between us after the man left with Lily and told her I've been looking for her.

She stepped back and my heart fell.

I told her how sorry I was and how stupid I felt after rejecting her but she was hurt and I couldn't blame her.

I was still trying to get things right when Alpha Miles arrived. How didn't I hear the gate.

He approached us and frowned then asked me why I was still around.

I got angry at that question and told him I was here for my mate and that I will be taking her with me.

He yelled, saying I rejected Alyssa and she is not going anywhere with me and that finally solved the puzzle.

He knew all along that Alyssa was my mate that's why he lied about her not being in this pack and why he never wanted me lingering in his house.

We got into an argument until Alyssa shouted at us both to shut up.

She walked towards me and asked me to leave saying she didn't need me there right then.

I was really pained by her request.

Her phone rang and her expression after that got me worried.

Alyssa's Pov

My hands started shaking as the kidnapper ended the call.

Tears slipped from my eyes and Axel rushed to my side.

"Are you okay Aly?" He asked and I shook my head, more tears spilling down my cheeks.

Miles rushed to me and gripped me from Axel's hold, making me wince.

"I ask that you leave now because my Luna isn't feeling too well today." Miles said.

"Lies. She's my mate and our bond never got broken so she can't be your Luna!" Axel yelled and I held my head.

My son had been kidnapped.

I didn't know what to do.

Yet these two kept fighting and it was killing me.

I didn't have time for this.

I quickly ran into the house to get Anthony. He was the leader of the pack warriors and probably could help in finding my son.

I met him in the dinning room with Mila and Sara.

Both women rushed to me and enveloped me in a hug.

"Oh dear, I heard what happened, we're going to find our prince soon." Mila said while I broke into another round of tears.

As we all separated from the hug, I noticed Miles and Axel ran in after me.

"Miles, why is he...." Mila was referring to Axel as his presence here was unusual.

She put two and two together and realized he must have finally seen me.

"Anthony I need your help, Kian has been kidnapped." I said to Anthony who had been quietly watching us.

"What?!" Everyone yelled simultaneously.

"Yes. The kidnapper called." I said, my voice breaking. "My poor son."

"That Lawrence! He must be behind this. I knew that peace meeting was just a mere distraction. He wouldn't give up that easily!" Miles yelled and hit the wall angrily.

"Kian is your son?" Axel suddenly asked and only then did I realise my mistake.

"Give me the kidnapper's number." Miles said purposely dismissing Axel's question.

I immediately complied and he dailed the kidnapper's number.

"Fuck it's unreachable!" He yelled in frustration.

"We'll have to wait till he calls back." Anthony said.

I sat on the dinning stool and started crying.

"My poor baby. I don't even know how he's doing."

Miles sat beside me and patted my back.

"We're going to find him. I'll make sure of it." He said.

"If Kian is your son, then-"

"He's our son. We had him together. So you can leave now." Miles said interrupting Axel.

I didn't know what to say. If I denied his claim, Axel would find out that Kian was his son and that could create more complications, especially now that Kian was missing.

Worse, he might take my son away from me and that I couldn't afford. So I just said nothing.

Axel looked hurt.

He went silent and just kept staring at me.

"I don't believe that." He finally said.

"Then go to hell." Miles said and Axel suddenly lunged at him.

Next we all knew, they were at each other's throat.

Anthony tried separating them, then my phone rang.

I left the dinning room and answered the phone.

'If you want to still see your son, meet me now at the Pack's boundary.' the deep voice said and the call ended.

I froze then looked back to the dinning room to see they were still yelling at each other with Anthony trying to hold Axel and Mila doing the same for Miles.

Why were they both being so immature? My son has been kidnapped for goddess sake!

Without thinking twice, I turned and ran out of the house.

I'm going to save my son.....

>>>>>>>>>>>Hey Lovelies

Hope you enjoyed the chapter. Please leave your answers in the comments and vote please.

15.Ultimate Power

Allysa's POV

I went to a nearby bush and transformed into my wolf.

I ran as fast as I could to the pack's boundary. On Getting there, I noticed a dozen guard wolves and hid behind a tree to change back.

Putting on the clothes I had in my mouth, I walked towards the wolves and they bowed to me in respect.

Everyone in the pack treated me with respect because Miles told them to.

It made me uncomfortable at first, considering the fact that I'm not truly from this pack.

But I've gotten used to it now.

"Let me through, I need to be somewhere." I said and they all exchanged looks before one who I think was their leader approached me.

"I'm sorry but Alpha wouldn't allow that unless you're with him." He said and I sighed.

I had to get across. My son's life was at stake here.

"I promise, it would be quick. Just let me-" before I could finish my sentence, gunshots were heard and all the guards suddenly fell flat, dead.

I screamed in horror and placed my palm over my mouth in an attempt to suppress my screams.

I looked up to see the culprit and four large men, dressed in black and all wearing masks approached me.

"Who...who are....are you?" I asked shakily.

I still couldn't digest the fact that the men I was talking to about a minute ago were now all dead.

"You want to see your son right? Then you better come with us." One of the men said and before I could respond, I blacked out.

Axel's Pov

I couldn't accept the fact that my mate might have had a child with Alpha Miles.

No,I didn't believe it.

Any sane person would see my resemblance to that pup and Alyssa probably just hated me right now and that's why she wouldn't tell me the truth.

"I don't believe that." I said and the bastard told me to go to hell.

I lunged at him furiously and we broke into a fight.

"Can you both just stop it?! You're both fucking Alphas yet acting like a child! For goddess' sake the woman you're both fighting over has disappeared!" Mila suddenly yelled making us halt pulling out each other's throat.

"Where did she go?" Alpha Miles asked panicked.

"We couldn't notice cos we were busy trying to separate you two." The pregnant lady who had been quite since I got here said.

"Anthony look for her upstairs." Alpha Miles said and Anthony obliged immediately.

"I'll look outside. Mila look around this floor." Alpha Miles said again and ran out.

Mila also left leaving just I and the pregnant lady.

"I know you've made a mistake by rejecting your mate and you must have realised that too. I'll tell you this. Alyssa loves Kian dearly and she'll do anything to protect him.

If he has been kidnapped by an enemy pack, he should be there. Alyssa also knows that and therefore she must have gone to get her son.

Make your amendments quickly and go save your son." She said and left.

I blinked twice, registering all what she said and sprinted out of the house.

I bumped into Alpha Miles outside but didn't stop running.

I transformed into my wolf and ran as fast as I could towards the Pack's boundary.

That lady was right.

Alyssa must have gone to save her son at cross moon pack.

On reaching the Pack's boundary, my suspicions were confirmed.

Those bastards must have intruded. They killed so many innocent wolves!

My Alyssa must be in trouble. I need to save her.

I ran so fast without a break. Crossmoon pack was an hour from here and I'll make sure to get there just in time to save my mate.

Alyssa's Pov

I opened my eyes slowly and registered my environs.

I was tied on a chair in a small, very dark and stuffy room.

The only available source of light was from a small window on the ceiling.

The room reeked of dried blood. This must be a toture room.

The door opened and in came a fat, short old man.

He grinned at me and I almost puked just at the sight of his decayed tooth. The room bit brighter now that the door was opened.

"Hello beautiful." The man said in a really gruff voice.

"Who are you?" I asked.

"Haha. You're a really funny one. You cut straight to the chase, no time to spare huh. Haha." He laughed animatedly.

In my opinion, he was the funny one. He was laughing when nothing was funny literally.

"I'm Alpha Lawrence. I'm sure you must have heard about me from Miles boy and my men did pay a little visit to you once." He said and I scrunched my face.

Was he referring to the day I saw a shadow by the window? He must have been scheming this for long.

"My son and I have done you no harm. You have an issue with Miles not me!" I said suddenly frustrated.

"Hahahaha. I really said it that you wouldn't be as boring as the rest." He said and sat on the chair before me.

How did I not notice the chair before now?

"You see, all these years of my life, I've been destroying Packs just to expand mine. Killing useless Alphas just to gain more power.

I mean you couldn't blame me as a mateless wolf."

What was he ranting about? He was destroying Packs and killing innocent people just because he didn't have a mate?

"And you really think if your mate saw all what you've been doing, she'd appreciate that?" I tilted my head and he stood up angrily.

"She died! Because of the useless Alphas she died! I needed to gain power to avenge her death. I was so weak, I couldn't protect her. Do you even know the pain of loosing your mate?!

Oh I'm sure you do after all your mate rejected you!" He yelled and I looked down. Did he have to mention the part of my mate rejecting me?

"Now I'm so powerful, but I won't stop until I've wiped out every single Alpha in existence, until I've gained the ultimate power!" He said and started laughing hysterically.

Was he been serious right now?

"Not while I'm still around, fat soul." I looked up immediately at the sound of my mate's voice.

I couldn't believe it, my mate was really here!

>>>>>>>>>Hey Lovelies

Sorry for the late update. Hope you enjoyed this chap Please vote and comment

Love you all, byeee

16.A Promise

You're a beautiful person if you're reading this

Pov

I got to cross moon pack and fought off the guard wolves at the border, making my way straight to the pack house.

I changed back to my human self and wore a pair of basketball shorts I saw along the way.

I felt my mate's presence the moment I arrived at the pack house and traced her scent.

Following her scent, I ended up at a basement. That bastard must be hiding my mate there.

I encountered a couple wolves who tried to fight me but I killed them within ten seconds.

Getting towards the door I heard my mate's melodious voice.

"And you really think if your mate saw all what you've been doing, she'd appreciate that?" I paused listening attentively.

"She died! Because of the useless Alphas she died! I needed to gain power to avenge her death. I was so weak, I couldn't protect her. Do you even know the pain of loosing your mate?!

Oh I'm sure you do after all your mate rejected you!" I frowned at that.

Did that bastard really have to worsen things. I was trying to make amendments and here he was....

"Now I'm so powerful, but I won't stop until I've wiped out every single Alpha in existence, until I've gained the ultimate power!" He continued and I smirked.

What a fool.

"Not while I'm still around, fat soul." I said making my grand entrance.

I loved the look on my mate's beautiful face on realising her saviour was already here.

"You, how did you get in here?!" Lawrence asked stomping towards me.

"Release my mate and son now." I said ignoring his question.

"Hahaha. In your wildest dreams. Guards!" He yelled and four men ran in. Were they there the whole time.

I smirked.

This is gonna be fun.

The first one lunged at me and I easily threw him off to the end of the room.

"Axel." My mate breathed clearly worry about me and I nodded at her in reassurance.

In a few minutes, all four men went unconscious.

"Impressive. Now I see why you're one of the greatest Alpha. Too bad I'll have to kill you!" Lawrence said and ran towards me.

Was he being serious right now?

Before he could get to me, I moved sideways and he fell to the ground.

"Argh!!!" He squealed.

I ignored him and went to untie my mate.

"Are you okay?" I aksed genuinely worried.

Her eyes went glossy and she nodded slowly.

"Kian. They still have him." She said and I nodded.

I turned towards Lawrence who was rising on his feet.

"You wrench!" He yelled, holding his left elbow.

"Where's my son?" I asked.

"You'll never see him again!" Lawrence yelled and I sighed.

This old man was being difficult and I was feeling stressed already.

"Fucking. Tell. Me. Where. He. Is." I gritted.

"He's in the execution room and in exactly 10 minutes, his head will be separated from his body!" He said and laughed hysterically.

"What?! No! My poor son. We have to save him, Axel." Alyssa said holding my arm.

I took her hand and we both ran out of the room,

We somehow found the execution room within five minutes and true to his word, Kian was tied up on a table, a large metallic sharp-edged machine slowly coming down his neck.

It was exactly four minutes left till the object met his neck.

"Kian!" Alyssa cried and tried running to him but I held her.

"There's a bomb attached to him. If we touch him, it might explode." I said motioning to a small tick bomb attached to his left arm.

"Oh no, my poor baby. Please Axel. We have to save him." Alyssa said.

I walked towards Kian and carefully cut the ropes tying him up.

It was a minute left.

I cut the wires of the bomb carefully, making sure not to make any contact with the bomb.

It went off immediately and I sighed in relief and quickly carried my unconscious son just before the metallic object could snap his neck.

Alyssa ran to me, crying at the same time smiling.

"Thank you so much for saving my son." She said and reached out to hold Kian.

"Why didn't you tell me about him?" I asked as she held Kian tightly.

"I didn't want you rejecting him like you did to me." She said not looking at me and I sighed.

"I'm really sorry Aly. I was so young and foolish, I didn't realize what I was doing at that point. Believe me every single day after that have been a toture. I tried my very best to find you but.....in all, Aly I'm truly sorry." I said.

"I'm gonna need time Axel. And I really hope you can give that." She said and I nodded solemnly.

As long as she gave me a chance, that could work.

"Would she at least introduce me to my son then?" I asked and she looked up.

"I guess Kian would love to meet his dad." She said and I smiled.

I took Alyssa and Kian back to blue stone pack against my will.

I really wanted to take her home already but I knew I'll have to give her time to forgive me first and I'll do everything to make that happen as soon as possible.

Alpha Miles was jealous when I brought Alyssa and Kian back. He obviously wanted to be hero here but he had to understand that Alyssa was my mate and Kian my son.

It was my responsibility to protect them.

He has been doing that in my stead for a while but now I'm back, I didn't need him to so that anymore.

Kian was still sleeping and Alyssa went to bathe him. The poor kid had been through a lot.

That Lawrence bastard. I made sure to deal with him nicely before sending him off to the bureau of justice.

With that old bean out of the way, I only had my mate to deal with.

I'll make sure to get her back at all cost and that's a promise.

>>>>>>>>Hey Lovelies

Hope you enjoyed this chap, pls vote and comment

17.Goodbyes and Introductions

You're a beautiful person if you're reading this

Pov

"And done!" I clapped as Kian stood up and started jumping in happiness.

It has been two days since Axel came to rescue Kian and I and so far everything has been going smoothly.

I could tell Miles was upset when I told him about Axel's request to know his son but I wasn't about to keep my son from his father especially now that Axel genuinely wanted to meet Kian.

Axel was coming later today and I'll officially let Kian know his Dad.

"Now I'm a pro at this." Kian said as he sat back down beside me.

We were mastering his counting and my baby did so good.

"Of course baby." I said and kissed his cheek.

"Mommy."

"Yes my prince?"

"Is Uncle Aiden really leaving today?" Kian asked and I looked up at him.

"What? Leaving where?" I asked him.

"Uncle Aiden told Lily and I that he's going to find his path." Kian said and shrugged before picking up his activity book and crayons.

I scrunched my brow in confusion. Aiden was leaving? I needed to talk to him.

"Baby stay here, I'll be back soon." I said and Kian nodded not sparing me a glance. Whatever he was colouring must be more interesting than me.

I smiled and patted his hair before leaving his room.

On my way out I bumped into Miles.

"Hey, hey. What's the rush?" He asked and I smiled weakly.

For the past couple days, there have been some kind of tension between Miles and I.

"Is Aiden really leaving today?" I asked.

"Oh I did forget to tell you about that. Aiden wants to explore, according to him. He said his wings felt clipped here and who am I to stop him?

I've been looking after him since his parents died ten years ago. I guess it's about time I set him free." Miles said and I nodded.

"I'll go speak to him." I said and set of to Aiden's room. I couldn't believe him. Was he really planning on leaving without telling me?

I knocked on his door and it was opened swiftly.

"Princess." He grinned and I folded my arms, keeping my face straight as I clearly wasn't happy with him.

"Oh come on. You know what they say, don't turn the twinkles to wrinkles." He said and laughed heartily.

I smiled at his cheekiness. Was he ever going to grow up?

"I'm pretty sure you just made that up." I said and he stopped laughing.

"Alright to what do I owe this visit?" He said and practically dragged me into his room before shutting the door.

I sat on his bed and looked around. He really was packing up alright.

He sat on a chair opposite me and place his chin under his palm, grinning at me.

"You are leaving and didn't think it was necessary to tell me right?"

"Oh boy. I saw this coming." He said and stood up.

He looked towards the window, backing me.

"Listen Princess. It was a decision I've made a long time ago but only had the guts to tell anyone recently. I knew you'd be upset if I told you and you were so fixated on your mate and finding Kian. I really didn't want to add to all that." He said then turned to me.

I could see his eyes were becoming glossy. Was Aiden really about to cry?

"Still, you should have told me. That's what I'm here for, to listen to you and support you at all times. If Kian didn't tell me about this, you were really planning on just leaving without a good bye?" I asked and he shook his head vigorously.

"No princess. I'd never do that. I was gonna tell you eventually." He said.

"You know, I would have left a few years back. But I grew attached to you and Kian. It was really difficult making this decision but it's something that's gonna make me happy. If my parents were still alive, I'm very sure they would have supported me on this. So please Princess, give me your blessings so I can embark on this new journey of my life." He said and I didn't know when we both started crying.

I gave him a hug. A long heartfelt one.

If this decision was going to make him find happiness, then I had no reason to stop him.

Aiden left later that day and everyone felt it.

The house was definitely different without Aiden. I missed him so badly.

I was presently in the kitchen trying to bake away my sadness while Mila and Sara assisted me.

"Your mate is coming this afternoon right?" Mila asked measuring the baking powder.

"Yeah. He should be here any moment soon." I replied focusing on the eggs I was cracking.

"I'm excited for Kian. He's going to finally meet his dad." Sara said smiling and I also smiled.

It's true I was still very mad at my mate for rejecting me but I was really glad Kian was getting a chance to meet his father.

Sometimes I'd see the look in Juan's eyes whenever he saw Lily playing with Anthony and I knew my son wanted that too. But Kian being the sweet and lovely kid he was will never voice out those thoughts.

He seemed to understand that his father had hurt his mother.

"Alyssa, Alpha Axel is here." Greg informed me walking towards Sara.

"Oh." I muttered and quickly washed my hands.

"Mila please take care of these." I said and left the kitchen.

I opened the front door and saw my mate talking to Kian.

It was such a sweet sight and at that moment I felt contented.

"Mommy!" Kian yelled on noticing me and ran to hug me.

Axel looked at me smiling. I blushed a bit and focused on Kian who was practically glued to me.

"Kian we have something to tell you." I said when Axel approached us.

"What's that mommy?" Kian asked looking between Axel and I.

"Alpha Axel here, he's-"

"He's my daddy right?" Kian said and my eyes widened in surprise.

How did he know that?

>>>>>>>>>>>>Hey beautiful people. I really hope you enjoyed reading this chapter as much as I enjoyed writing it

I'm pretty excited for the next. Please don't forget to vote and leave your thoughts in the comment section.

Love you all, bye

18.Let's see you try

You're a beautiful person if you're reading this____

Pov

I stared at my son still surprised by what he said.

"How do you know that?" Axel came to my aid, squatting beside me so he could reach Kian's height.

He held Kian's shoulders as he spoke to him.

"I heard Aunt Mila and Aunt Sara talking about it. And I look so much like you so I figured it out." Kian said.

His smartness amazed me and sometimes I feared it was a little too much for his age.

"Mommy never smiles whenever you're around or someone mentions your name. I know she hid in her room at Lily's party because she didn't want to see you. You must have hurt mommy a lot that's why I never asked her about you." Kian continued and my eyes started watering.

My son was so sweet and compassionate, thinking about his mom before himself.

I kneeled beside Axel and drew Kian to myself.

"My baby." I said then hugged him, sobbing silently.

I hugged him so tightly, trying my best as possible to bottle up the swirling emotions inside me.

"I'm sorry." Axel said. I could hear his voice breaking.

I pulled apart from Kian and rose to my feet. Axel also stood up.

"Ian, why don't you say hi to your daddy?" I said smiling down at Kian and he smiled back before turning to Axel.

"Hello, daddy." He said so cutely, I felt my at warm at that.

Axel smiled like he had just won the biggest price before lifting Kian in his arms.

"Hello son." He said then rubbed Kian's hair and kissed his forehead. Kian hugged him and he did the same.

I didn't ever picture a moment like this but right now I knew I'd always want this to go on forever.

I've made the right decision by letting Kian get to know his father.

++++++++++++It was evening already yet Axel refused to go home. He had been playing all day with Kian in his room and I was getting worried for Axel because it was already late.

I knew I really didn't have to worry because he was an Alpha male and he could protect himself but I still was.

Now Axel was drawing animals with Kian. They were both so immersed in their own world to even acknowledge my presence.

For once I felt neglected by my son.

I smiled as I watched both of them squeal at the success of what they had drawn and hug eachother.

It had been years since I saw this playful and carefree side of Axel.

A part of me still loved Axel and it was a fact I couldn't deny. With time I could find it in me to forgive him and maybe go back to him......

"Mommy!" Kian suddenly yelled and ran to me.

I smiled at him as he sat beside me on the sofa and hug me.

"Mommy can I go with daddy?" He said breaking the hug.

I looked between him and Axel who was still sitting at the play area watching us.

"Uhm I don't know about that baby. We never discussed about it." I said and Kian's face fell.

"Pretty please mommy. Why don't we both go with daddy and be just like Lily and her parents. Uncle Greg also lives with Aunt Sara in the same room and they'll be having a baby soon. Shouldn't we be like that too?" Kian said and my heart stung.

Axel stood up and walked up to us.

He kneeled before me and held my hands.

"Buddy, why don't you go find Lily. I need to talk to your mommy." He said and Kian obliged and ran out of the room.

"Aly listen, I know I've fucked up and it's gonna take some time before you forgive me but look at me Aly, I'm trying, trying to be the best for you, trying to make things right again.

Think of our son, he needs both of us, together as a family. Please Alyssa, come back home." Axel said and a tear slipped from my eye.

"I told you before Axel, I'm gonna need time." I said and took my hand from his, wiping my eye.

"I know but-" He was interrupted by a loud cry downstairs and we both ran outside to see what was going on.

Sara was standing in the living room holding her large bump. Her water broke!

Greg was by her side looking very confused.

"We need to get her to the hospital." I told Greg.

"I'll go get the car." Seth said and left.

Seth, Greg and Sara went to the hospital in one car while I went with Miles.

I had Axel go home and he said he'd be back the next day. I couldn't really argue with him plus Kian was crying as he didn't want to be separated from his Dad so soon.

I was starting to get jealous that my son seemed to love someone else as much as he loved me.

Mila and Anthony stayed at home with the kids.

Sara was in labour for an hour and a smile appeared on my face when I heard the beautiful cry of the baby.

Minutes later, we were allowed to go into the ward to see the newborn.

It was a very cute baby boy. I couldn't feel much happier for Greg and Sara.

Sara was discharged and we all returned home.

Kian and Lily couldn't seem to keep away from the baby, everyone absolutely loved this new baby who had been named Garrett.

The next morning, I assisted the maids in making breakfast for the family.

While we were all having breakfast, the doorbell rang and a maid went to get the door.

"Daddy!" Kian yelled, leaving the table and running towards the front door.

Axel was here so early.

"He acts like he now lives here." Miles scoffed and bit harshly on his pasta.

"Come on Miles. He's here for his son." Mila said and Miles glared at her.

Axel approached us and greeted us.

Everyone replied casually except Miles but the reason for that wasn't a puzzle anymore.

"I'm taking Kian home today." He announced and Miles suddenly stood up.

"Let's see you try."

>>>>>>>>>>Sorry guys, I know the chapter title is lame. Didn't really have one for it so

Anyways hope you enjoyed the chapter. Vote and comment pls.

Love you all, bye

19.Going back home

A xel's Pov

I parked my car outside and entered the compound whose gate was unlocked.

Miles must have a lot of confidence to leave the gate open.

I headed towards the front door and rang the doorbell.

A maid opened it and bowed respectfully.

I nodded at her and walked towards the dinning room.

Kian called out to me and ran to hug me.

I carried him and approached the others at the dinning table.

My eyes immediately went to Alyssa. I greeted casually and everyone replied casually except Miles.

Not that I cared anyways.

"I'm taking Kian home today." I announced and Miles suddenly stood up.

"Let's see you try." He said glaring at me.

Oh hide me, I'm scared

I thought sarcastically then smirked at him.

"Oh? I'm sure Kian would love that and Alyssa has no problem with that. Right Aly?" I said looking at Alyssa who seemed conflicted.

I couldn't blame her though. She must feel obliged to respect Miles and his decisions after all he took her in when she left unwanted the most.

But I wasn't having that. She was my mate and I'd make sure to make everything the way it should be. She and Kian should be back home with me, not here.

"I.... I. Uhm. If Kian would like that, then I guess it should be okay." She said, trying her best to avoid Miles's gaze.

"Aly, you can't just agree to let him take your son. What if he doesn't return him? What then?" Miles said.

"That's not going to happen because I'll return to take Alyssa too." I said and everyone stared at me surprised.

"What do you mean by that?" Alyssa asked and I smiled at her.

"Kian can't live without him mother and you can't do that also and I definitely cannot live without the both of you, that's why I've decided we should all live together at my pack, where you both rightfully belong." I said Mila made an awwn sound.

"Yay!!!" Kian jumped and clapped happily.

"You see. Even Kian agrees with me." I said. Alyssa was still looking taken aback.

"Or better yet, why don't she go now? That'll be greater!" Mila suggested.

"Yeah I think so too. Then Alyssa you can come visit us whenever." The woman who went into labor yesterday said.

"Both of you just shut up. Alyssa and Kian are not going anywhere." Miles frowned.

"Miles everyone knows you have feelings for Alyssa and that's why you don't wanna let her go. But I think it's right to allow her go to her mate." The gamma spoke for the first time and i was surprised.

"Greg you seem to have forgotten how her so called mate hurt her." Miles said.

"But he's sorry now, Miles." Mila said.

Alyssa suddenly stood up.

"Why don't you all ask my opinion before making conclusions for me?" She said, her voice breaking.

"Aly I-" I couldn't finish what I was about to say because she left the dinning room.

Miles was about to go after her but his Beta, Seth held his hand.

"I think you should let her be." He said.

"Daddy let's go to my room, I'm done with breakfast!" Kian yelled and pulled me away without waiting for my reply.

When we got upstairs, he led me to the room beside his instead.

"This is mommy's room. You should talk to her and convince her to come home with us." He whispered and I smiled.

My son really got my brains.

"Okay but why don't you come with me so we can convince her together?" I whispered back to him and he nodded happily.

We entered the room and saw Alyssa lying on the bed.

She noticed our presence and sat up.

"Mommy!" Kian yelled and ran to hug her.

"Baby." She hugged him tightly. I went to sit beside them.

"Aly." I called out slowly and she turned to face me.

"Listen I'm sorry for making a decision without your knowledge." I started.

"You hurt me Axel, and as much as I'm trying to forgive you, it's not easy. You need to give me time Axel." She said.

Kian was looking between both of us.

"I know, but it's really difficult. I've been apart from you for too long and I don't think I can survive anymore without you." I said and looked down.

A tear slid down my face.

"Please forgive me Aly. I've been punished enough." I said.

I felt a hand on my face wiping my tears and looked up at my mate.

I held her hand and kissed it.

"Please forgive me, I can't live without you anymore. No, I can't live without both of you." I said.

"I forgive you." She said.

"You mean that?" I asked and stood up.

"Yes I do. I think I had forgiven you for a very long time." She said again.

I hugged her so tightly and Kian also joined in the hug.

It was such a sweet moment.

"Thank you so much Aly."

++++++++++++Alyssa announced to everyone that she had forgiven me and she'll be going with me to my pack. I couldn't be any happier.

Everyone seemed okay with it and they were already saying their good byes.

Miles was unhappy though but he had no say in this. It was Alyssa's decision and he had to respect that.

"Is your pack really the biggest in America?" Kian asked while we were packing his stuffs.

"Hmm hmm" I replied smiling.

"Cool! So I'm going to be the Alpha of a very large pack?" He asked again and Alyssa chuckled.

"Yes cutie." I replied and he jumped happily.

Then he suddenly became sad.

"What happened?" I asked.

"Then am I never going to see Lily or baby Garrett again? Bummer, I was just getting to know him." He replied and Alyssa gasped.

"Kian, where did you learn such words?" She asked.

"Uncle Aiden." Kian shrugged and I chuckled.

"Good grief, Aiden!" Alyssa mumbled annoyed.

"Don't worry Kian, you can always visit this pack." I said to him ruffling his hair and he tried taking my hand off.

I tickled him and he laughed hard.

This was a moment I wanted to last forever.

>>>>>>>>>>Hey lovely people. I really hope you enjoyed this chapter.

Finally Alyssa forgave him!!!

Sorry Miles and Alyssa's shippers□

We're coming to an end of this book and I'm really grateful for your love and support so far. Please keep voting and keep those comments flooding in!!!

Love you all

20.Now until Forever

You're a beautiful person if you're reading this________________________________

Pov

I said goodbye to everyone with an heavy heart.

I thanked Miles for all he did and promised to be back sometime.

Though he didn't want me to go, he knew he had to let me go for my happiness.

I got into Axel's car continuously staring back at the place I called home for the last five years.

I'd forever be grateful to them all.

I couldn't believe I'll be returning to my old pack.

What was it like now?

Would I still be welcomed there?

Did anyone even remember me there?

"Put on your seat belt." Axel said breaking me from my thoughts.

I nodded and put on the seat belt then looked behind to see Kian was carefully tucked on a car seater.

Wow he even got a child seater ready for Kian.

"Is it really okay for me to go back?" I asked while we were already on the road.

"Of course. Why would you think about something like that?" Axel said his eyes fixed on the road.

"I don't know, maybe because I felt they wouldn't want me back." I said staring at my shoes.

The car suddenly came to a halt and I looked up at Axel.

"You have no idea Alyssa. Everyone has been searching for you. We all regret everything. Neglecting you when you needed us the most.

We all realised we were foolish for blaming you for your parents' death. It wasn't your fault at all. We should have been beside you to comfort you while you were grieving." He paused then looked back at Kian who was fast asleep.

He turned to me again and held my hands.

"You were so young yet we blamed you for everything. It must have been such a heavy load to carry." A tear slid down my face and he wiped it.

"We're going to make up for every single day we didn't treat you right. You're my mate and Luna of Blue Moon pack and the whole world is gonna know that." When he finished he kissed me on the lips then continued driving.

I was shocked for a minute then blushed profusely.

His words were so sweet and reassuring and I knew for a fact he meant every bit of it.

I hadn't made the wrong decision by returning to him. Nala was also very happy at this new development.

It took a few more hours till we reached Blue Moon pack.

Everything still looked the same only that some new buildings were added and the bushes unbelievably greener.

This pack was full of life and buzzing. It was the largest pack after all so you couldn't expect less.

My heart raced as we approached the pack house.

It looked the same as I could recall.

Axel parked his car and carried a sleeping Kian out of the car.

It was already dark but Kian slept throughout the trip. I was worried he would be too active tonight.

I carried Kian's luggage and backpack while Axel carried my luggage.

The front door opened as we approached it and I saw Kian's parents and sister Bianca.

They all looked shocked but happy to see me. They took turns to hug me, telling me how sorry they were and gushing over Kian who woke up with all the drama.

We had dinner together with me being the main subject.

After dinner, everyone retired to their rooms. I went to my old room and tears filled my eyes as I reminisced on my memories of this room.

"The room was always kept clean and none of your stuff were moved." Axel sais behind me. I noticed too, the room was just as I left it.

"Kian can sleep here and you'll sleep in my room." Axel said and I turned to him.

"It's fine, I'll sleep here with Kian." I said blushing.

Axel looked down at Kian who was looking between both of us.

"No mommy! I like my privacy." Kian suddenly said and ran into the room and closed the door immediately.

I stared at the door in shock.

"He really is my son." Axel smirked and I frowned.

"You're teaching my baby bad stuff." I complained and Axel pulled me to him. Sparks went flying and I blushed profusely at the close contact.

His head went to my neck, taking in my scent.

"Axel I... I." I couldn't complete my sentence because Axel crashed his lips on mine.

It was such a passionate and fiery kiss. I let him take control and soon my legs felt weak.

He held me firmly and pressed me against the door, continuing his toture on my lips.

My mind went back to our first night together, all the passion I felt that night.

"I want to mark you right now." Axel said huskily. His eyes had turned completely black and I knew his wolf had taken over.

I nodded slowly and he didn't waste another second before digging his fangs into my neck.

++++++++++++++I squinted my brow as I tried to adjust to the bright light in the room.

I was held tightly by a muscular body and I struggled to get out of Axel's grip.

I sat up on the bed and smiled down at him. He looked so peaceful while he was asleep.

I drew the duvet closer to my naked body and winced slightly at the pain I was feeling down there.

My mind immediately went back to last night.

After Axel marked me, he led me to his room and took off my clothes and his.

"I've longed for this so badly, Aly. Let me have you tonight." He told me and I nodded shyly.

He started kissing me but then I stopped him.

"We still need to tuck Kian to bed." I said then he paused for a moment as if communicating with someone through the mind link.

"Bianca is on it." He said and went back to kissing me.

Back to the present, I blushed as I remembered the event of last night. Though this wasn't our first time, it really felt like the first to me.

I traced every angle of his face and his eyes fluttered open.

I gasped and drew my hand back but he quickly held it and placed it on his face.

"Why are you scared mate? I'm yours just as you're fully mine so you are free to touch what's yours." He said in a really sexy morning voice and I blushed yet again.

He sat up then kissed me. I felt self conscious because it was morning and my breathe must stink.

"I love you Aly." He told me and I smiled.

"I love you too Axel."

"I promise to be with you, love you and protect you now until forever." He said and I hugged him.

"That's a promise."

....

The End

www.ingramcontent.com/pod-product-compliance
Lightning Source LLC
Chambersburg PA
CBHW070406200726
48294CB00003B/1120